Promises

AN AMISH LOVE STORY

Shepherd's Crook Publishing
7295 Wadsworth Road
Medina, OH 44256-7406

KATHRYN MILLER HOLLOPETER

ILLUSTRATED BY CHARLOTTE SIGMON

ISBN 1-890050-01-6

Dedication

To my husband, Glenn

PROLOGUE

The first Amish to sail to the new land had come in the early 1700's and settled first in eastern Pennsylvania along with Mennonites and Brethren and certain other groups who had been called Anabaptists (Rebaptizers) in Europe back in the sixteenth century. Their reforms went farther than those of Luther. They agreed with him that salvation is by the grace of God, conditioned on faith alone and not by the mere partaking of sacraments. But they did not believe infant baptism to be scriptural. They believed each person by his own decision, at an age when he can be accountable to God must repent of his sins and be baptized as a believer.

So they rebaptized adults who chose to join with them and who had been automatically baptized as infants. To the state church, whether Lutheran or Catholic, this action was seen as an affront to their authority. The Anabaptists were considered heretics. A peace-loving people, they would not join the state military. Locked in prisons to die and rot, drowned in rivers, burned at the stake, their lands seized by the authorities, thousands of them chose martyrdom rather than giving up their faith.

They were hounded into the hillsides of Switzerland, and forced to hide in the forests of France and Germany giving up their lands and possessions. The movement spread like wild fire, as the state authorities tried harder to put an end to it. Finding comparative rest in Alsace-Lorraine, a region on the French-German border, many finally settled there for a time. Tired of being harassed, they withdrew from the world around them becoming exclusive and were known in some places as "the quiet in the land". One leader, Jacob Ammon, in particular insisted on separation. His group, nicknamed Amish, resisted change in almost every area of their lives such as styles of dress, their habits of worship, their language and new inventions. During certain periods they banned, or shunned, those who left their group. Finally, in America, they found freedom to worship without fear of harassment by the government. From their first settlements in eastern Pennsylvania, some migrated farther west to Somerset County, north to New York and south to Virginia. Continually increasing in numbers, and always needing more land for the next generation, many followed the frontier to Ohio, Indiana, Ontario, the Dakotas, Oregon and Kansas.

So, in 1810, ninety-nine years before our story begins, several families had moved into the hills of Holmes County, Ohio, and had begun a settlement there which soon grew into a large self-sufficient community. Some German Lutherans and French Catholics had settled among the Amish in the early years. They worked alongside them, sharing in harvesting, in building, helping each other in any time of need, but there was not the same bond of standing together as one people which the Amish people shared. The persecutions of the state churches in Europe had not been entirely forgotten.

Instead of erecting elaborate church edifices, they met in the homes of the members. In the summertime the upper barns served well as a place of meeting. During cold winter months, benches that were transported from place to place were set up in the house where the meeting was being held.

The Amish looked askance on anyone in their group who deviated from their practices; independent thinking was not considered a virtue among their own people and only fostered pride. But they were fascinated by any suggestion of absurdity in outsiders. They depended on each other within the community for most of their needs, producing their own food, clothing and even their carriages which were patterned after the hackney coaches, but without a seat outside for the driver.

The bishops had decided that the modern changes which were coming, they were better off without. The clothing styles need not be constantly changing, better to stick to the simple ways. Consequently the Amish held on to a style of clothing that peasants had worn for centuries in Europe. Years before 1909, when bonnets had come into vogue, the Amish women had begged to change from the hats they had worn to their own style of bonnet. Now that hats with their plumes and flowers were back, the bishops insisted on keeping the plain, homemade bonnets for summer and heavier overcaps for winter. Because buttons had a connotation to military uniforms, hooks and eyes were used on men's jackets in lieu of them. Still today, women fasten their dresses with pins. There are exact designations for each article of clothing, for how men's hair should be cut, the growing of beards without mustaches, etc. There are slight variations from district to district and group to group such as allowing or not allowing rubber tires on some farm machinery. They can not always tell you why things are done a certain way, only that they've always been done that way. What was good in the past should not be too quickly changed or discarded. As Thomas Carlyle, the Scottish essayist and historian, wrote: " All great peoples are conservative; slow to believe in novelties; patient of much error in actualities; deeply and forever certain of the greatness that is in law, in custom once solemnly established, and now long recognized as just and final."

As has happened in many churches or movements that began in a spiritual fervor, the strict adherence to the Bible that the Amish began with, may have over the years fallen into a religion of many man-made rules and of the importance of good works. Nevertheless, to this day this group of people are quick to come to the aid of their fellowman and do not spare themselves to help materially those who suffer in times of natural disasters. They are careful not to misuse the land and other resources God has given them and remain an asset to any society they choose to live among.

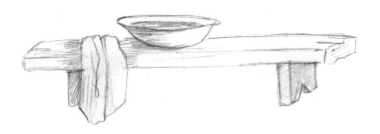

CHAPTER I

Andrew Yoder's ears still rang from the noise of the steam engine and the threshing machine. Now there was only the sound of the crickets and the katydids calling to their mates. He spread his blanket on a pile of new straw up against the stack in the barnyard, and stretched his lean, muscular body out on its crisp softness. His hair was damp from his dip in the creek after supper. A soft breeze drifted across the stubbled field stroking him with its coolness. Lying on his back he watched the stars coming out. The sliver of moon hung low in the sky as the last rays of color faded away. Nearby his brown horse grazed, his four white feet deep in clover.

It had been one of those sweltering hot days in mid-July when the sun shines constantly, and night comes as a relief. In the afternoon billowing thunderheads had suddenly mushroomed above the hills casting a foreboding darkness. It had looked as if the threshing might be ended for the day. Rain could be seen coming down in white sheets across the hills on farms a mile away. The lightning had crackled and thunder shook the earth, but the clouds had moved off to the east and minutes later the sun came out leaving everything here as hot and dry as before. The threshing crew, with help from the neighboring farmers, had finished at Jacob Hershberger's that day. Ready to leave early in the morning, the threshing machine and the steam engine stood by the lane.

Simon Coblentz had been doing the threshing in these parts for years moving from farm to farm during wheat and oat harvest. Andrew, having recently come back to his home community, had hired out to Simon for the summer. The summer had begun uneventfully enough, but he enjoyed his work. With abandon he threw his energy into whatever he was asked to do.

1

He had often heard the stories of the early settlers who came to this area from western Pennsylvania in 1810, of how his own great-grandfather, John A. Yoder, had cleared a quarter section of land and built a log cabin on it. It was through hard work and faith in God that his people had built a community where they could raise their families and earn an honest living. Their serious dedication to duty and obligation to parents and to the community of faith was passed on from generation to generation.

Andrew had not concerned himself greatly with the idea of getting married, although his mother had reminded him occasionally that he was getting on in his twenties. When he had left her early the past Monday, she had admonished him, half joking, "Now keep your eyes open, Andy. There must be a lot of nice Amish girls in Eli Troyer's district."

"Like there were forty years ago, huh, Mem?" he had teased her because it was the area in which she grew up. He had saved a little money over the years, but didn't feel ready to think of marriage.

Andrew heard Simon talking to the horses as he put his bedroll down in their stall. Tomorrow they would be moving on to thresh John Weaver's wheat. As long as the weather held out a few more days, they could finish up in the neighboring farms north of Walnut Creek. Then they would move the rig to Andrew's brothers' farms northeast of Mt. Hope.

Except for three years in which he had worked on his Uncle Isaac Yoder's farm in Indiana, Andrew had spent all his life in this Amish community of eastern Holmes County, Ohio. Now that his cousins were old enough to help with the work, his uncle no longer needed him. He had come home when the planting was finished the past June, and had hired out for one dollar a day with Simon Coblentz on his threshing crew for the duration of the wheat and oat harvest. When threshing season was over, he planned to help his older brother, John, when he needed him for haying or husking corn on the family farm. There was always work to be done. When the farm work slowed down in the fall, he would get work at a sawmill.

His mind went back to his trip home on the train, the bustling station with its variety of people; the dandies in dashing suits talking about baseball and about an automobile race someone was making around the world;

2

the women with their plumed hats, their cinched waists and their mincing steps. The women *he* knew did not wear silly frills and put on airs. He had steadfastly ignored the two sophisticated ladies who had cast eyes at him from across the aisle whenever he looked their way. He was not interested in a superficial, temporary relationship. Nevertheless, it was exciting to have the attention of the pretty girls, and now he remembered the subtle scent of perfume with tantalizing pleasure.

As sleep crept over him, he felt secure in being back with his own people where he knew everyone, and they knew him and his father and grandfather and many more generations before him. His people had come to this valley in 1810, ninety-nine years ago. The quiet hills, with their little farms and villages and here and there a little family graveyard tucked in among them, created for him the most impregnable fortress in the world. Here his people could live their simple lives that baffled the shifting ways of a changing world.

By nine o'clock next day the sun was already shining hot; the dew had evaporated and the men were hard at work at John Weaver's. Some of the neighbors had brought their draft teams and their wagons. Some had come with just a pitch fork to load the sheaves onto the wagons in the field. Abe Mast's big brown team trotted in from the field with the first load of sheaves. He slapped the reins against their backs, and they strained to go up the bank into the barn, the wide oak boards creaking under the weight.

Popping and huffing, the steam engine began turning its pulleys and belts; and the threshing machine started its loud banging as it spewed fresh, golden straw into the barnyard, where twenty-year-old Peter Weaver arranged it into a round, airy stack. Grandfather, Peter Miller, sacked the grain while the younger Weaver boys, Benjamin and Joseph, dragged bag after bag to the granary, yelling orders to each other above the noise. Young Joe Mast pitched sheaves into the great gobbling monster until his wagon was empty. Then out he went to get another heap while a waiting wagon pulled alongside the threshing machine to unload. Thus they kept the wagons coming and going hour after hour.

Simon stoked the fire under the boiler from time to time, sweat rolling down carving white streaks on his smoke-blackened face. Andrew oiled

3

cogs, checked pulleys and tightened belts, making sure the noisy threshing machine ran smoothly as it pounded and broke away the stems and chaff from the kernels.

At noon John Weaver, who had been directing the straw out the doors of the upper barn, sent word out to the field, calling a halt to the work and announced time for dinner. The noisy machinery was shut down. The men laid down their pitchforks and began filing towards the house with anticipation, vigorously whacking the dust from their denim pants and their blue, homemade shirts with calloused hands. Near the pump, on a worn wooden bench, sat a row of white graniteware basins where they took turns washing the dust from their weatherworn faces and arms.

Louis Ravel had come as a neighbor, too, to help with the threshing. He in turn would receive help from his Amish neighbors on his small field. He was one of a handful of Catholics who lived in the area and attended the little church just outside town. When he came from France as a young man, the Amish community in Walnut Creek was already well established. He had always gotten along well with his neighbors, and having grown up with them, he took no offense at their exclusion of him in personal matters and quite expected it.

Louie kept to himself much of the time. Almost seventy-five years old, he still farmed his eighty acres with the help of one old horse. A buggy stood in his barn, but he seldom used it. He loved walking into town, stopping to watch the blacksmith at work or sitting on a bench exchanging stories with his friend, Andre. On Sunday mornings he could be seen early walking up the road to the little church. His Amish neighbors were kindly indulgent toward him during harvest, but he was aware of being set apart, an outsider in their midst and seldom a part of their social events.

At noon the work horses had been given a portion of oats and hay and watered at the trough. A retired racer, Andrew's horse was a road horse and not used in the fields. The young man glanced at him cropping grass in the barnyard. He found himself walking beside Louie, behind the other men on their way to dinner. The threshing machine had been shut down, but its din still rang in their ears. A thin layer of chaff covered the ground, the trees and the roofs of the chicken coops. Several hens, scratching for

4

fallen grains, scattered as the men walked through. "Do you think the weather will hold out a few more days?" Andrew ventured amicably.

"*Oui.* Is good weather for harvest. But rain is needed for the streams so the cows and calves can drink." Louie was a short man, but muscular. Rumor had it that in his younger days he had once lifted a tree sixteen inches in diameter off a man's leg when they were cutting logs.

"You got nice horse," said Louie, "fastest horse around they say."

"Prince is pretty fast. He was a race horse once. He's good in the sulky," replied Andrew modestly, turning to observe his horse.

"You ever ride him?" The Frenchman spoke with an accent, but Andrew did not find him hard to understand.

"Yes I do ride him a lot. When I got him, he didn't like to carry anyone on his back. He had a habit of biting. Must've been mistreated before I got him. He would reach back and try to grab my leg. Almost got it a couple of times. But I broke him of the habit and he is very gentle with me now. Don't know if he would let anyone else ride him, though."

"A horse can know a man's mind," Louie responded. "If the master is gentle with him, the horse will be gentle. I loved to ride my horse when she was younger, but she is getting too old to go very far."

"Time to get a new horse, Louie," Andrew laughed.

They washed their faces, splashing water on their dusty arms and necks. Elizabeth Weaver came down the porch steps with fresh towels on her arm. Andrew recognized her as John Weaver's little Lizbet, but how she had changed in the years since he had come with his mother to visit the girl's grandmother. She had grown from a little tomboy into a demure young lady. Ringlets of light brown curls escaped from the blue scarf tied tightly around her head. Her eyes were shyly downcast in the presence of so many men. The thick lashes lifted as she handed Andrew a towel. She smiled in surprise, recognizing him. "Hello, Andy."

"Hello, Elizabeth, how are you?" he answered, fascination written on his face. But she had already turned and run up the steps, her skirts twirling slightly showing bare, brown ankles.

The Weaver household had been a beehive of activity for days. The feast put on for threshers in Amish farm homes surpassed all other feasts throughout the year except the bountiful meals prepared for weddings. The bounties of the Ohio countryside were not squandered by these industrious people. Blackberry and sour cherry pies and loaves of bread had been baked by the dozens in the outdoor oven the day before, wasting their glorious smells on the summer air. Beans had been baked overnight; kettles of summer apples gurgled on the stove for sauce. Early in the morning Sarah and Elizabeth had caught four squawking chickens and dressed and stuffed them for roasting.

The good aromas coming from the kitchen door tantalized the hungry men. Plump, rosy Susanna (known by everyone as "John Suzy") was illustrious as one of the best cooks in the region, and would not be outdone by any of the neighbor wives on threshing day. She came to the door now and signaled to her husband that all was ready.

The men and boys marched in removing their broad-brimmed straw hats at the door and jostled each other for places on benches positioned around the heavily laden table which had been stretched out as long as possible. The best china had been brought out. Susanna, arms akimbo, surveyed the sumptuous fare to make sure nothing was missing down to the last pickle. Twenty-one-year-old Sarah came in with a large platter of steaming, smoked ham saved for the occasion. Last came a dish mounded high with mashed potatoes, mouth watering streams of browned butter trickling down creating little pools of titillating promises. There was considerable juggling to find room for them among the pickled beets and eggs, the tangy cabbage slaw, cucumbers in sour cream, slices of hearty yellow cheese, and homemade jellies and butter to go on the thick slices of bread. Anna, just turned nine, was stationed near to chase the flies from time to time with a piece of folded newspaper.

The chatter died down, and everyone grew silent for a minute as heads were bowed in thanks. The women hovered in the background ready to refill a glass or replenish the plates of chicken and ham, noting with pride how the food was passed and consumed with obvious enjoyment. There was little conversation as the farmers concentrated on the business at hand.

Joe Mast took pleasure in the subtle teasing from his friends, the nudgings under the table and snickering whenever Elizabeth came near to refill a plate. It was common knowledge that he had set his cap for her, and the teasing was to him an affirmation of his chances. The girl took no notice of their boyish insinuations, but when Andrew held up his glass and winked at her, she blushed and spilled the water as she hurried to fill it.

When the men showed signs of being sated, the desserts were brought in; the pies, the delicate lemon sponge cake and the puddings. The dinner ended with another silent prayer followed by a great scraping of chairs and boots on the wooden floor. As the farmers filed out grabbing their hats, they nodded their approval to the cooks, some adding a word of praise. They sighed, patted their bulging bellies and threw themselves down in the shade to rest and give their stomachs time to recover.

Andrew flung himself down and pulled his hat over his face for a snooze. Nearby a cluster of men were talking in subdued voices in the low German dialect which was used exclusively among them except when reading the Scriptures or in prayers. His curiosity was kindled as he heard snatches of the conversation.

"How much money is missing from the mill?"

"A hundred dollars!"

"When did Dan have it last?"

"On Monday afternoon." The mill belonged to Dan Miller, John Weaver's brother-in- law.

"Someone saw him walking by the mill late, when it was getting dark already," said Jacob Herschberger in an intimate tone. "I don't know, but it looks suspicious." He pulled menacingly on his pipe.

"These Frenchman have strange ways; you don't know what to expect of them," added Abe with a sidelong glance toward Louie who was leaning his back against the porch, his eyes closed, oblivious to the conversations around him having little understanding of their language.

John Weaver stood among them, his feet spread, his bronzed arms folded across his chest. His broad shoulders spoke of years of plowing and harvesting. Not so quick to form an opinion about others, and of a more tolerable nature, he interjected, "He seems like a good enough man to me. We've never had any trouble with him."

7

"Those are the ones you have to watch out for," warned Eli Troyer, bishop of the area, casting his eyes around for assent.

"No, I don't believe it was him," insisted John, walking resolutely away.

Andrew was aghast with disbelief. They were talking about Louie, blaming him because he was not one of them. At least John Weaver had not gone along with their suspicions.

The steam engine began its loud chug-chugging as Sam fired up. A huge cloud of black smoke glided into the air. The men rose and sauntered toward the barn taking up their tasks where they had left off.

Before evening chore time, the neighbors took their teams and went home to milk their cows and slop their pigs. Several of them would be back next day to finish John Weaver's wheat. They would be done before noon; then the rig would be set up at Louie Ravel's to thresh his small field.

Simon and Andrew oiled the machinery and got everything ready for the next day. His task finished, Andrew stood looking out the upper barn doors surveying the peaceful panorama. He was delighted to see the Weaver girls coming to the straw stack below with clean bed ticks to fill with fresh straw. Sarah and Anna held the large ticking sack, while Elizabeth tried to stuff it full of the stiff, rustling straw. Unaware of their observer, they giggled and teased, pushing each other down into the scratchy, golden pile; until Sarah, being the oldest and more serious, said, "Come now, we've got to get these finished. Mem will want help with the milking, and the menfolks have to be fed again, too!"

"The way they ate today, you wouldn't think they'd need any tonight," Elizabeth laughed.

"Stuff it real tight, Lizbet," exclaimed Anna, holding a corner of her own smaller tick. "I want my bed to be up to the ceiling." And they thought about how the beds felt each year after threshing when they were high and stiff and new.

"Leave a little straw for me to sleep on tonight," teased Andrew.

The girls looked up startled. "How much does it take for a man your size?" retorted Elizabeth.

Laughing at her tart reply, he answered, "Just enough so a man can get a good night's rest after overeating at that wonderful dinner!" And leaping down onto the straw pile, he slid down the stack before the astonished girls.

They let him help them finish and carry the ticks to the house, where Susanna was busy tightening the ropes that were stretched on pegs across the bed frames to hold the straw mattresses. Andrew hoped for a chance to talk more to Elizabeth, but the girls had their chores to do, and work came first.

The next day, Saturday, Louie's ten acres of wheat were finished by early afternoon. They got the machinery ready to go, and Simon went off with it to the Mt. Hope community to begin again Monday morning, providing it didn't rain.

Andrew offered to help Louie take his wheat to the mill. The old man was glad for the help. His back was feeling the strain of harvest more than in his younger days. He invited the young man to stay with him for the night, and Andrew gladly accepted. He had hoped to stay in the neighborhood until Sunday evening so he could participate in church activities. It was his mother's childhood community, and he knew many of the people. Church meeting would be held at Abe Mast's, just across the field from the Weavers' farm. The church in his community would hold meeting the following Sunday. The two friends loaded the bagged wheat on Louie's rickety wagon, keeping enough back for seed for the following year and a little for his dozen scrawny chickens.

The old mill had been Dan's father, Peter Miller's. Peter and his wife, Veronica (known as Franey), now lived in the "Grossdäddy" house between the mill and the Weaver farm. Their daughter was Susanna Weaver, Elizabeth's mother.

Peter was a tall, sturdy man about seventy years old, and he still loved to putter and help around the mill which had made him a prosperous man. He and the Frenchman had been friends for years. He greeted the men as they pulled up in their wagon.

"How goes it? Have you got good wheat this year, Louie?" he asked, puffing on his pipe.

"Biggest crop in a long time, thank God," answered Louie crossing himself. The two old men shook hands.

"This must be Sam John's Andy," said Peter looking at Andrew and referring to his father and grandfather as the people often did to designate which Andy or John or Levi. The same names were repeated over and over from one generation to the next. Andrew's father had been called Yon Sam's John.

Andrew held out his hand, noticing the twinkle in the eyes of the old man, not unlike those of his granddaughter, and was pleased that he had remembered him. Dan came out of the mill white with flour from his eyebrows and beard to the toes of his shoes. He measured the grain and paid Louie in bills and silver coins, one hundred and fifty-five dollars which Louie put in an old leather pouch he pulled out of his pocket. The remainder of the pay came in sacks of ground grain which he would use to feed his animals through the winter.

Peter watched them drive out of sight. "It wonders me why the young man is with the Frencher," he muttered. "John told me that Abe thinks Louie took the money that's missing," he said to Dan who was locking up. "That Abe is always so suspicious," he said throwing back his head and laughing.

"It's doubtful, but then, you trust everybody," Dan needled. "He walks by here almost every day," he said, taking his coat from the hook behind the door and locking it.

Back at Louie's Andrew rubbed down Prince and fed and bedded the horses while Louie milked his two cows. It was nearly dark when they finished eating supper. They sat in the dark kitchen talking and sipping the wine Louie had brought out.

"It's a nice little farm you've got here, Louie. How many acres have you?"

"Eighty acres my father got when he came over from the old country. Forty I farm; the rest is in woods and pasture. *Oui*, the land gives me everything I need. But I miss my Octavia," Louie ended pensively.

A loud rap that rattled the screen door startled them. Louie pushed back his chair, and wiping his mouth on his sleeve, walked slowly to the door.

"Wonder if you could tell me how to get to Sugar Creek?" The tall stranger spoke curtly, shifting his feet. A shadow of dark stubble on his chin gave him a sinister mien.

"This road takes you straight in," answered Louie waving his hand toward the south. He could not see the stranger's face clearly in the shadows, but observed that he was carrying nothing with him. His store bought clothes were in a shabby state as if he had spent the nights sleeping outdoors.

"You got anything to drink around here? I'm mighty thirsty. Must have walked twenty miles," the stranger said in a rough voice.

Louie motioned toward the pump in the dooryard. "There's a tin hanging right there. Help yourself."

After gulping several cups of water, the stranger stalked up onto the porch, swung the door open and strode past Louie, his heels thumping on the bare floor. "Now, if you'll spare me a bite to eat, I'll have to be on my way."

"Sure, don't know why I didn't think of it myself." Louie pushed the dishes back making a place for the man at the table. "I don't have nothing fancy," he said good-naturedly, but we don't go hungry."

The stranger made no reply. He had taken no notice of Andrew, but sat with his back to him and kept staring out the door. Andrew did not like his surly manner, but being a peaceful man, he waited to see what would happen. He had never used a gun and didn't know if Louie had one. The stranger shuffled his feet impatiently.

Louie sliced potatoes and poured them sputtering into the hot frying pan. He set out a jug of fresh milk, still warm; some cold boiled eggs and a plate of coarse dark bread. Still glancing furtively at the door, the stranger bolted his food greedily.

"Do you live here all alone?" he said abruptly. His black brows scowled menacingly, and yet he had not said anything unkind.

Louie did not mention the young man sitting in the shadows, but answered, "*Oui*, ever since my wife, Octavia, died four years ago."

"How far is the nearest railroad station?" asked the ominous stranger, rising to his feet.

"Must be about ten miles. It's right as you come into Beach City."

"There should be a train going west some time tonight," the man said as if to himself.

"You don't have to leave tonight. I don't have an extra bed, but if you don't mind sleeping in the barn, you're welcome," Louie offered hospitably, giving the stranger the benefit of the doubt.

The sinister man moved closer towering above him and lowered his voice intimately. "If you can spare me a few dollars now, I'll be on my way and much obliged."

"Well, I can't spare you much, Louie answered slowly, it's got to last me the winter, you know, and I have my taxes to pay. Would two dollars do?"

"Where do you keep your money? Go and get it!" the stranger commanded pulling out a pistol.

Louie felt numb for a moment. He blinked his eyes, picked up the oil lamp and started for the bedroom with the stranger dogging him. He realized that he had spoken foolishly but was glad he had not involved the young man. Lifting the mattress, he pulled out the leather pouch he had tucked in there just that afternoon. The coins jingled as he untied the strings and began sorting out two silver dollars. The man reached for the bundle and took it with, "I'll handle that!"

"Sure," Louie said, shivering as he realized what was happening.

"Now if you don't squeal on me, you'll get your money back, see? Think you can keep quiet if I don't tie you up?"

"*Oui*, I won't tell no one, not a soul," Louie promised through chattering teeth.

Just then Andrew moved out of the shadows. The stranger was startled and raised his gun, but Andrew put him at ease by offering, "Would you like to borrow a horse? Seems a pretty far piece to walk at night." The man looked bewildered for a moment. He started out the door. Louie opened his mouth to object, but Andrew sent him a look that the old man understood.

The dark man turned, "It would help, if you've got a good gentle one."

"Got one as gentle as a girl. He's fast, too. I'll saddle him for you as

12

soon as I get a lantern."

The stranger kept his gun raised. Andrew saddled Prince stroking the brown velvet nose and patting the smooth neck as the stranger stuffed the leather pouch into one of the saddlebags. He talked soothingly, running his fingers through the black mane while the man mounted. The horse cringed slightly, his eyes darting apprehensively to and fro, but he stood obediently still.

"Now start him out slowly, and he'll do better for you. I don't know for what, but he doesn't like to cross that bridge down the road by the mill. Just kick him in his belly a few times and he'll go."

The robber impatiently grabbed the reins which Andrew handed to him and started briskly down the road. The two men stood in silence for several moments watching him go. Finally Louie exclaimed, "*Douleur, douleur*, my money is all gone! What will I do now?" He stared down the road in the direction the robber had gone. "But I am forgetting, my friend, that your horse has a habit of biting. Do you think he will bring the man back?"

"We'll have to wait and see what happens," Andrew answered. "You go to bed and don't worry about your money. I'll sleep in the barn and keep an ear open." He walked to the stable, blew out the lantern, lay down on a pile of straw under the manger and fell asleep.

It seemed like only minutes later when a buggy clattered into the yard. Louie's light was still burning. There were men on the porch talking to Louie. When Andrew stepped up behind them, he recognized Jacob, Abe and Bishop Eli.

"What do you want?" asked Andrew.

"The sheriff is looking for a man who tried to rob a store in Walnut Creek tonight. He got away. They think he has a gun." Abe Mast paused for breath. "Jake's wife thought she saw a strange man walk up this direction about dark."

"So you thought you would check here?" asked Andrew, anger rising, and not waiting for an answer he went on. "Well, was he tall, or short like Louie here?" he demanded sharply.

"We told you, it was getting dark already, and she couldn't tell what he looked like," answered Jake hotly.

Andrew scowled. "There was a man who came by here tonight. Louie and I had just gotten finished with supper when this stranger knocked on the door and asked for a drink and a bite to eat."

"Well, where is he?" the men asked crowding closer.

"I gave him some supper," Louie spoke up, "nothing fancy, but that man sure ate like he was hungry! Then he wanted to borrow some money."

"You don't mean you gave it to him!" Abe interrupted.

"What else could he do? The man had a gun!" Jacob reminded them.

"I'll get it back,though," Louie said, glancing at Andrew.

The farmers snickered and looked at each other knowingly. "Well, which way did he go from here?"

"Andrew gave him his horse to use. He wanted to go to the train station. He seemed pretty tired to go that far so late in the evening," Louie said taking no notice of the looks the men exchanged.

The neighbors looked at Andrew questioningly, with shocked unbelief. He nodded his head. Louie had told the truth. They climbed into their black surrey shaking their heads half in amusement, half in pity. "Let us know when you get the money back," one of them sneered as they drove off.

As Andrew was walking back to his straw bed, he heard a familiar whinny. Prince had run across the field and now galloped up to him and nuzzled his pocket for a treat. The young man petted and praised him; then reaching into the saddlebag and pulling out the pouch with the money he handed it to Louie who broke out with a stream of French, waving his hands as he jumped up and down, the coins jingling. *"Merci,merci!"* was all that Andrew could understand.

The horse was put back into the stall and unsaddled. The old man was still in a frenzy of excitement as Andrew calmly soothed Prince, brushing and currying the sweaty, dusty coat. Sleep had left them and they busied themselves about the stalls.

Suddenly Eli appeared at the barn door. *"O du Gott,"* he exclaimed, "so that's where the horse went. Never would have believed it!" he said out of breath. "We found the thief in the ditch along the road down near the bridge, but no money, no horse. The man was unconscious. Jake and Abe took him to the doctor. There wasn't any room for me, so I said I'll walk home. His one pant leg was torn clean off at the knee, but we couldn't figure out what had happened. Now here's the horse!" he finished, throwing out his hands.

"Here's the money, too," said Louie, holding up the worn leather pouch and shifting his feet in a little dance.

"But what happened?" asked Eli impatiently.

"Well I was pretty sure he wouldn't get very far on *that* horse," said Andrew. "Prince has a bad habit of biting any rider in the leg if he doesn't like him, and there wasn't much to like about this man. It was obvious he had never ridden a horse before."

The bishop shook his head and slapped his knee, hilariously pleased at the outcome.

"Is the man seriously hurt?" Andrew looked anxious.

"Nah!" answered Eli. "He was coming to already."

Louie had a sudden thought. "Say, I promised him I wouldn't tell no one about the money, but I just let it slip before I thought. I guess it won't matter now, anyhow. Maybe it learned him a lesson!"

"You got the money back, and there wasn't any shooting, no harm done," Eli said as he started down the road, impatient to share the news with somebody.

Andrew lay awake a long time thinking over the eventful day. The stir of the evening was over. Now he could turn his thoughts to what he'd had to push from his consciousness all the busy day. He had found the young Weaver girl very appealing, and quite to his surprise, he found himself scheming ways in which he could assure himself a chance of talking to her after meeting next day. He had never felt like this about a girl before. The old man snored in the next room as Andrew drifted off to sleep.

CHAPTER II

Church meeting was being held in Abe Mast's barn. Sarah and Peter Weaver had gone with the grandparents; Susanna had made sure that the younger ones were dressed and clean. With deft movements she had braided the little girls' hair tightly, dipping her hands into the basin of water from time to time, her fingers making a squeaking sound as they slid down over the brown strands. Benjamin, Joseph and Annie climbed into the back of the surrey that John had brought up to the gate, while little Fannie, Veronica's namesake, scrambled in front between her parents.

Elizabeth had left a little ahead of the rest, choosing to walk across the fields and through the woods. Her father's farm was a quarter section that her great-grandfather had homesteaded. The land sloped pleasantly to the south to a little valley through which Goose Creek meandered. Here is where he pastured his cows and horses.

She followed the stream until she came to where a large, flat rock rested in the middle of the water. The run was never dry, being partially fed by the spring that bubbled out of the hillside near the house. Many years before, someone had built a little springhouse over it. Inside, the moss-covered walls were always cool. The trough through which the spring water flowed, held crocks of butter, tubs of cream and milk, and leftover dishes of meat.

Gathering her long, blue skirt, Elizabeth jumped onto the rock, then to the opposite bank. Her mother had often told her she had long legs like her grandfather, Peter Miller. Sometimes she wished to be small and dark like Sarah, who was quiet and poised, and never seemed to get into the predicaments she did.

17

For almost a year Sarah had been keeping company with John Hershberger, who came calling Saturday nights. Their families understood that the young couple would be married in the winter when the butchering was finished. But no one else would be told until the bans were announced two weeks before the wedding.

Elizabeth did not lack for beaus among the boys in the neighborhood, but treated them with disdain, relishing her freedom. Abe Mast's Joe was one who had pursued her with unflagging zeal. On Saturday evenings at dusk he had come through the gate and crept to the door only to find himself locked out. He fancied himself quite a catch, and if he had known that Elizabeth herself turned the bolt, he would certainly have taken it as an affront to his ego.

Susanna was chagrined at her daughter's disinterest. "Why don't you like Joe?" she asked bluntly. "He's a nice, hard working fellow. Good looking, too. He'll probably get his father's farm one day."

But Elizabeth, having heard her mother list her requisites for a husband many times had learned to dismiss her without argument, unconvinced, her own list of desirable qualities intact. Though she could not have articulated her thoughts on the subject, in her heart she sensed when a man had maturity and sensitivity. She thought of Joe still as the arrogant boy who had teased and pestered her all through their school years, always feeling it necessary to prove himself the fastest, the smartest, the best at everything.

As for Andrew, she remembered the strange excitement she felt when their eyes had met, the glow that had crept over her when she perceived how he set her apart from the others with small attentions. Elizabeth wondered when she would see him again. Trips more than eight or ten miles outside their home communities were infrequent.

She had reached the top of the hill in the pasture and sat down on a stump to rest. For the past two weeks she had been hired girl to the Herman's, a Lutheran family in Walnut Creek, helping take care of Mrs. Herman's mother who was bedfast. The need of her help in cooking for the threshers gave her the happy fortune to be at home a few days. Remembering the constant dirty linens, the hacking and drooling, made her doubly thankful to be out in the fresh air with the clean wind on her face.

A crow swooped by, cawing raucously, and perched in the top of a tall oak. The song Mrs. Herman had played on their new Victrola kept going through Elizabeth's mind. It was a worldly song, and try as she would to forget it, it wove itself through her thoughts like the ribbon appearing and vanishing in Annie's hair.

"After the ball is over,
After the break of dawn,
After the dancers' leaving,
After the stars are gone...."

Elizabeth stopped to gaze over the valley. There was their farmhouse with the summer house beside it, the spring house, the milk house and hen houses; and watching over all, the big, white barn with its new yellow straw stack. Over the tops of the trees below, she could see the roof and the water wheel of Uncle Dan's flour mill standing weathered in the sun. Not far away stood his house with the little *Grossdäddy* house close by. Across the valley and up the hill north of her home, squatted the little schoolhouse where Joseph and Annie attended in the winter. Her elders had been talking about the fine new teacher who could teach the children "old" German which was the language of *Die Heilige Schrift*, and not like the low dialect of everyday talk. It was important that they learn to read the Scriptures. A pair of bluejays screamed, shattering the stillness. In the distance horses whinnied to each other as they turned into the lane at Masts' farm, the buggies rocking behind them. More were coming in lines down the road from both directions. A few people on foot walked in little groups along the dusty road. Elizabeth watched the tableau, intrigued by this new perspective. From the south by itself came a handsome horse with a sulky. The lone driver's hat was cocked familiarly to one side as he lounged easily in the seat. She knew immediately it was Andrew coming to meeting.

Realizing suddenly that she must hurry or be late, she jumped up from the stump that had been her stool and ran down the hill toward Masts' barn, deftly skirting clumps of brambles. Carefully she climbed over the fence and ran up the barn bank as the last people were taking their places

on the backless, wooden benches, the men on one side facing the women on the other. The upstairs barn floor had been swept clean, and there was a sweet scent of new hay mingled with the ever present smell of cattle and horses which being accustomed to, no one took note of.

Elizabeth pushed in unnoticed beside her sister and their friends looking slightly disheveled. Sarah gave her a wry look as she picked burrs from her sister's skirt and stockings. After a few moments Elizabeth raised her eyes cautiously to see if anyone had noticed her. Everyone seemed busily intent on himself or his neighbor except for one pair of gray eyes that smiled and held hers for a moment.

Now there was no more time for laughing and talking. The men had removed their hats as the *Vorsinger* announced the first song from the Ausbund and began the tune in a slow, sonorous intonation that resembled the Gregorian chants of the Middle Ages. *"O, Gott Vater, wir loben dich, und deine gute Preisen."*

Several preachers gave fifteen-minute discourses. Then Bishop Eli preached the main sermon; and starting with Adam and Eve he went through Joseph, Moses and Tobias, his voice rising and falling in a singsong, on and on. No one talked or moved about except when a restless child had to be taken out, or the young girls slipped out in twos and threes coming back to sit again as the sermon droned on. By the time the preacher got to Jacob and Esau, many people were already lost in their own thoughts of planting and harvesting, cooking, sewing and courting. The younger boys leaned on each other fast asleep. Finally the bishop announced the time for prayer, and everyone turned and knelt, leaning their elbows on the benches. The long prayer over, the people stood while another prayer was read from the prayer book, all genuflecting at the mention of Jesus.

At last the meeting was over. The men stood talking in little groups outside, waiting for lunch. Barefoot children ran in and out among their elders, the little boys in their straw hats and suspenders just like their fathers, the girls in their black caps and plain pinafores.

Lucinda Mast and her daughters set out the food on long tables in the summer kitchen; coffee and milk, bread, apple butter, cheese, pickles and half-moon pies. When the men had eaten, they went out while the women took their places.

Standing in a circle of men, Andrew was surprised to find himself the center of attention. News about the robbery had gotten around.

"That was something how you tricked the robber last night!" one of the men said , wiping the sweat from his forehead.

"The police and everyone are glad to have him in jail," offered another approvingly.

"He had a gun, but you outsmarted him without one," came from one of the preachers.

Standing with their fathers, the little boys looked up at Andrew with silent admiration.

"Where did the man come from?" someone asked.

"He said some things to the sheriff as he was coming to," answered Jacob Herschberger importantly. "Seems he may have been the same man they've been looking for, the one who tried to rob some farmers coming home from taking a load of wheat to Canal Fulton. Those fellows had guns, and he didn't get their wheat money, but he got away."

"He came up from Steubenville, they think," Abe Mast put in. "Well, they got him now. He'll be sitting in jail for quite a while."

"I wonder if he was the one who stole the money from the mill, too?" someone queried.

Dan Miller grinned sheeplishly as his brother-in-law, John Weaver, poked him with his elbow. "Katie found it in his overshirt pocket when he took it home on Saturday afternoon," John laughed.

"My overshirt hung behind the door at the mill all week," shrugged Dan. "It was hot and I didn't wear it much. When Duffy paid me for the load of flour for his store, I was busy and stuck the money in my pocket and forgot about it. Katie found it when she was dusting my coat yesterday evening."

"Since she found it," John interrupted, "I think Dan should give her some of it for new shoes or something." The men laughed with him and agreed that Dan should reward his wife with a new pair of shoes or some fine material for a dress.

Soon the adults and young children went home to rest and visit, and then to do the necessary farm chores. The young people stayed for the "singing" which would be held in the barn in the evening.

As the afternoon wore on, the young men lolled under the trees in the yard and talked of such things as horses, making small wagers on whose horse would win if they had a race. But it was too hot a day for races, and Andrew refused in any case, having a little ways to travel yet that night. His attentions toward Elizabeth had not been passed over by young Joe Mast who had noticed Andrew's eyes following the girl. Joe glared with disdain at this stranger from another district coming in to steal the girl all his friends knew he had staked out as his.

The day was growing cooler, and Joe suggested having a wrestling match as they often did. He usually being the favored winner, and not above illegitimate moves such as arm twisting, the other young men glanced at each other knowingly, reluctant to take him on. Finally David Troyer agreed to a match. They struggled, rolling over on the grass until Joe held his opponent down and was declared the winner. He leaned against a tree, out of breath.

"I'll rassle anybody that wants to," he challenged. "Come on. I'm not afraid of any two of you," he boasted arrogantly, his eye on Andrew.

"Go on, Andy," the fellows urged, hoping to see the braggart silenced.

"Give him a chance to rest," Andrew replied magnanimously, calmly eyeing his opponent.

The young girls came now with dishpans of popcorn, trays of half-moon pies and summer sausages. Cups of cool peppermint tea were passed around. The girls then spread quilts on the grass near the boys to sit and gossip, and to be an audience for their favorite members of the stronger sex.

Joe walked cockily to the center of watching eyes, confident that he would put his enemy to shame. Andrew rose slowly, rolling up his sleeves. They faced each other momentarily like bantam roosters, eyes glued, feet moving. Suddenly Andrew lunged and caught the younger man's leg throwing him onto the ground. Joe wrapped his legs around Andrew's and held his neck, pushing to get on top. Superior in strength as well as wit, Andrew, with a sudden spiral move, twisted free, and held his oppo nent to the ground while everyone cheered. They stood, Andrew holding out his hand, and Joe reluctantly giving it a feeble shake, vowing in his heart to get even for this humiliation.

The benches had been removed from the barn floor except for a few left around the perimeter. The slanting rays of the evening sun shone in at the open doors gilding the thick oak beams and delineating stray pieces of straw with a delicate light. The young people began to gather for their "singing". Johnny Herschberger started the group singing with several slow hymns in high German. As darkness began to fall, more young people from other districts gathered in, and the night air rang with faster, English songs, "In the Sweet Bye and Bye" and "Shelter In the Time of Storm". After a time there was an interlude; the young folks mingled and the evening took on the air of a party.

Two lively young men from Bishop Schlabach's district near Sugar Creek got out their fiddles and tuned up. The men and girls formed two lines to dance the Virginia reel. From the sidelines Andrew watched the graceful dancers weaving in and out, toes tapping, skirts flying. He had never seen dancing like this before.

Soon eight of the best dancers were persuaded to go to the center to show off their special aptitude. As the fiddlers sawed out "Turkey In the Straw", the onlookers sang and clapped. Joe made sure he was next to Elizabeth in the center. He smiled down on her triumphantly as he swung her around. He was an excellent dancer, and it was his chance to redeem himself. Round and round the dancers went, and from time to time Joe stole a glance at Andrew who was thoroughly captivated by the grace and beauty of the skilled young dancers whirling and gliding in time to the music.

When the dance was finished, Joe followed Elizabeth into the outer circle where they leaned against the oak walls of the granary catching their breath. Soon the caller began again, "Choose your partners," and the next tune started up. Joe pulled her along into the center to join the others who were lining up. Suddenly Elizabeth slipped out of his grasp and, darting into the shadows, left him wondering what had happened to her. She crept outside unnoticed and turned, startled, as someone appeared

24

beside her, gently touching her arm. "Elizabeth," he said her name softly. In the dull moonlight she recognized Andrew. "Where are you going, Beth?" he queried. "Home," she said resolutely.

"Had enough of dancing?" She did not answer, so he continued, "No need to walk home alone in the dark. I have to be heading home myself, and I will take you safely to your door on my way."

She did not object, but let him steer her to his horse and sulky, relieved not to have to walk home alone. The horse whinnied softly, impatient to be on his way. Andrew lifted Elizabeth easily to the seat which was little more than a board with no sides or back and with scarcely enough room for an extra passenger, the appropriate conveyance when racing. He swung up beside her and dangled one foot, bracing himself on the low dashboard with the other. Slipping his arm around the girl's waist, he held her tightly to keep them both from falling off. With a quick flick of the reins they rode off to the fading strains of " Skip to my Lou". When they got to the road, he let the horse trot, his hooves clip-clopping on the hard earth.

He turned south, taking the long way. She looked up at him questioningly, and he smiled back warmly, reading her thoughts. "It's still early, and such a beautiful night, don't you think?"

"Beautiful," she agreed, looking up at the moon.

To the west, black clouds were rising, the lightning dancing from one cloud to another. Andrew whistled softly as he let the reins fall limply in his hands. Elizabeth recognized the tune as the one she had heard at the Hermans', but waited to speak until he had finished the song.

"Where did you learn that tune?" she asked.

"I heard it in a cafe where I went to eat on my way home from Indiana," he grinned. The train was stopping to take on water in Topeka."

"After the ball is over," she began singing hushed, and wondered what Joe thought when he suddenly couldn't find her anywhere. She smiled to herself.

Andrew's masculine voice joined in, "Many a heart is aching," allowing himself to relish the thought of Joe's dismay at the turn of events. The two voices mingled in song on the night air and in laughter when the song ended.

Then all was silent again but for the sound of the horse's hooves and the wheels on the road. The wind began picking up unnoticed.

Intrigued with his travels by train she engaged him with questions, and he described the wonders of the iron horse, the interesting travelers, the sounds and smells of the steam locomotive.

But he was more interested in learning all he could about her. "I told you where I learned the song. Now you tell me where you learned to dance so well," he demanded, looking down admiringly at the flawless skin and the slightly flushed cheeks.

She laughed, a demure but genuine laugh, not like the nervous giggles of so many girls. "My uncle, Johnny Miller, taught them to us the last time he came home from out West."

"Is he your mother's brother?"

"Yes."

"I'd like to meet your Uncle Johnny some time. Does he come home often?"

"It's been over a year. When the harvest is over in the West, I hope he will come home again."

Raindrops cut their conversation short. They had turned north on the mill road, and he urged Prince into a fast pace. By the time they reached the covered bridge, rain had started pelting down hard, and the wind was whipping boisterously around them. He brought the horse to a stop under the shelter of the bridge just as a bright bolt of lightning flashed, illuminating her frightened face for an instant. The thunder clap came close behind rolling off into the distance as another flash came, followed by another deafening clap. He drew her reassuringly closer as they sat in silence, not able to hear each other above the whine of the wind and the clatter of rain on the roof. In his calm bearing she relaxed against him trustingly, shivering a little from the raindrops that had dampened her back and head. Removing his jacket, he placed it over her shoulders tenderly, subtly aware of his fingers touching her arms, her hair.

After a time the thunder sounded farther and farther off, but the rain continued for some minutes. Then suddenly the half moon made an encore flooding the stubbled hills again with its enchanting light. The stream had risen and rushed noisily along under the bridge. Everything smelled of wet soil and fresh rain as they drove off. The horse trotted along briskly now, eager to get home.

Sorry that the evening was ending, Andrew dutifully stopped at the Weavers' door and lifted Elizabeth down from the sulky.

"Thank you, Andy," she said softly.

"I did it gladly," he answered. "I hope we can do it again soon, and then you must teach me to do those dances."

"I will," she promised, smiling as she turned to go.

He watched her with longing until the door closed behind her. Then he turned his horse swiftly toward home, whistling, "many a heart is aching, after the ball," and wondering when he would see her again.

CHAPTER III

Andrew was up at dawn the next day, ready to help Simon Coblentz set up to begin another week of threshing. His mother, Catharina, was already stirring about the kitchen, cooking graham (a whole-wheat porridge) on the oil stove. She had hoped her son would be home to spend Sunday with her; she had missed him during the years that he had worked for his uncle. He kissed her on the cheek and sat down at the table where she had set a place for him. He had grown into a man during the years he was gone. She studied his face, the frank gray eyes, the tousled brown hair, the firm jaw that set off a gentle mouth which turned up at one corner when he smiled. So like his father, she realized with a sudden stab of grief. Thankful she was to have him sitting at her table devouring his eggs and bread.

Her other children were all married and starting families of their own. John J. lived in the old farmhouse with his wife, Amanda, and three children and farmed the home place. Catharina lived in the little "*Däddy* house" next to the big house. Her husband, John S. Yoder (S. after his father, Sam), had built it for them when their son John got married. Her husband had died of typhoid fever five years before, when Andrew was only seventeen.

Two of her babies had died before she bore Andrew; she was doubly thankful for him. It had been a difficult labor, and she had feared losing him, too. But he had never been spoiled, maintaining an independent, inquisitive nature and thriving from his first lusty cry. He had been the joy of his father, working alongside him until his older brother took over the farm.

They had helped each of their children get established when they were

29

married. Andrew's two sisters had moved to their husbands' communities. His brother, Samuel, had received a farm next to the home farm. Catharina was hungry for news of her childhood environs. "You came in pretty late," she ventured.

"Meeting was at Abe Masts', so I stayed and went to the singing."

"Did it storm over that way?"

He nodded his head, "Yah."

"You didn't get wet coming home?" She had worried about him, staring into the darkness long after she had gone to bed.

"It started to rain just as I got to the covered bridge by the mill, so I waited there until the rain stopped. The lightning was close," he said, remembering the sweetness of Elizabeth leaning on his shoulder. His mother detected a faraway look in his eyes, and familiar with the territory, wondered why he had gone up the mill road. Not in a frame of mind to concern herself with that, she dismissed the thought. She did not even ply him with her usual questions about the kind and quality of food the women had cooked at all the places where Andrew and Simon had threshed. She always had wanted to know how the food had rated in each kitchen and especially wanted to hear about any new recipe. Andrew sensed she had a heavier matter on her mind.

She sat down and smoothed her apron about her knees. "Sam is not following the *Ordnung* any more," she blurted. "They have laid the ban on him."

Andrew sat in stunned silence letting her words sink in. She was speaking of his own brother. "Does that mean we have to shun him, too? What about his wheat harvest?"

The tears welling up in his mother's eyes were answer enough. Without the threshing rig and the Amish neighbors' teams and wagons to help, Sam Yoder's wheat would be left in the field to rot. Scraping the legs of his chair noisily on the wooden floor, Andrew stood. Catharina followed him outside.

The sun had started climbing, taking the chill off the morning. The trees and roofs shone, having been bathed in the rain during the night. It would be a beautiful day. The dogs barked as the sound of the steam

30

engine's chugging was heard announcing the arrival of the monstrous threshing machine.

"*Wie geht's*, Katie," Simon Coblentz greeted Catharina casually as she leaned on the picket fence, waiting to hear the plans for the day.

The men walked toward the barn where John Yoder came out carrying two buckets of frothy milk to be cooled in the milkhouse water trough. Coblentz looked up at the sun that was rising behind the trees. "Should be dried off in a few hours, think not?" he asked. "I think we'll open up about noon."

"It'll take the afternoon and all day tomorrow to do this job if all goes well," said John. His wife came out of the house. "You don't have to cook for threshers today, Mandy," he called to her. "We won't be able to start before noon."

Relieved, the women could now go on with their usual Monday chore of washing the clothes and still have time to bake bread and pies for the big dinner the next day. Amanda went into the wash house and started the fire to heat water. Later the baking would be done in there as well. The young woman swayed slightly as she walked, her belly bulging almost imperceptibly under her loose dress. It was the beginning of her third month.

Soon the gasoline engine could be heard popping and puffing blue smoke out the window as load after load was washed. By half past eight the first shirts ballooned in the breeze as they hung on the line drying. When John had gotten this new contrivance for his wife, his mother preferred to continue rubbing her clothes on the old washboard just as she had always done. But as time went by, Amanda had persuaded her mother-in-law to put her clothes into the big new tub with hers, where they sloshed clean with little effort, leaving the older woman more time with her flower beds.

Little Barbara and Katie came out of the house in their night gowns, rubbing sleep from their eyes, looking for their mother. When they saw their Uncle Andy, they ran toward him with shrieks of delight. He caught them up in his arms one at a time and swung them around. They clung to his legs and begged for more. Two-year-old Johnny came running, carry

ing his cup and crying for breakfast. His father picked him up laughing, gave him a drink of the warm milk and sent him to his mother. Andrew handed off his nieces with promises of games and stories in the evening. All day long as Andrew worked, the news his mother had told him, kept crowding into his mind. He was not able to reconcile himself to it.

He had heard of Amish families from time to time who had left their group and had joined one of the Amish Mennonite groups who had pulled away a generation before and had built meeting houses. This new group did not hold as strongly to the old ways. The bishops, fearing the breakdown of their close community, had gotten very strict about shunning those who left the brotherhood. That meant that at family gatherings his brother, Samuel, could no longer sit down at table with them. They could have no business dealings with him. He would have to be treated worse than an outsider.

He knew that Sam had some minor differences with the church, but didn't feel they warranted such extreme measures. When revival meetings were held at the Longenecker Mennonite meeting house, Sam and his wife had attended at times. Andrew had received letters from him telling of the preaching he had heard, of the need to repent and believe, of a faith beyond joining the church and keeping its rules. The elders looked on such thinking as a dangerous discontentment that would lead one astray. How could one be sure of salvation! One could only hope. To do more was arrogance.

Most of the youth waited until they had "sowed their wild oats" and were ready to settle down to marriage before they asked for baptism and formally became a part of the church. Being in his early twenties, Andrew was seriously considering "following after the church" and had spoken to Bishop David Kauffman about it. That meant he would be placed in a class of other candidates for a lengthy period of instructions in the doctrines and dogmas of the church followed by the ritual of baptism.

Breaking the ban by helping his brother would generally be considered a disobedience to be repented of and could disqualify him for church membership. But how could it be a sin to help his own brother? His mind was in turmoil.

When the noisy machinery was shut down for the day, Andrew went to Simon Coblentz. "Guess we'll be moving over to Sam's when we're finished here," he said in a matter-of-fact way, feeling the older man out.

Coblentz didn't answer immediately, but kept his back turned, fastidiously checking the belts on the steam engine. "We're moving to Hochstetlers' next."

"But why aren't we doing Sam's threshing while we have the machinery here in the neighborhood?"

Coblentz shifted the wad of tobacco in his cheek and sent a stream of brown juice from between his teeth into the dusty grass. "The ministers' word, he is no longer one of us," he answered with pain in his eyes.

Stunned, Andrew formulated a plan in his head. "Could I have a few days off after we're finished here?"

"Yah, sure," replied Coblentz amiably. "Tell Sam it spites me. You know how it is." Andrew could tell he was genuinely grieved.

After supper Andrew saddled his horse and rode over to his brother Sam's. Sam opened the door. He was a tall, bearded man, ten years Andrew's senior. The children were in bed; Emma was rocking the baby. The men exchanged pleasantries. Then Andrew asked abruptly, "How do you figure on getting your wheat crop in? You know that Simon is not going to thresh for you?"

"I was expecting that," Sam answered. His eyes followed his wife carrying the sleeping child to his crib in a corner of the room. She paused to soothe the little one as he stirred momentarily. She was a slender, pretty woman; but she had an air of strength about her.

"I thought if we could haul the wheat into the barn, I would try to rent Simon's threshing rig after the season is over, and we can thresh it ourselves," suggested Andrew. "He has given me a few days off, and I think I can borrow John's wagon and team."

"Andy, I don't want you to risk your standing with the church for our sake."

"I have no misgivings about it. In my heart I know it is what I want to do."

34

"It will be hard work," Sam objected. But there was grateful relief in his voice.

"Isaac and I can help load the sheaves, and young Andy can watch the little ones," Emma said, offering her help and the help of their children. She sounded resolute, as if that closed the matter. Sam regarded her lovingly.

"I'll be over with the team tomorrow as soon as it dries off," Andrew said as he stood to leave. The two brothers gripped each other's strong hands, and Sam's eyes brimmed with gratefulness.

They gave Emma the easier job of driving the team and wagon while one man walked alongside pitching the sheaves up to the other who stacked them carefully to make a sturdy load. Young Isaac helped wherever he was needed and ran errands. When the younger children got restless, eight-year-old Andy would bring them to the field to sit under a tree along the fence row where they could watch their elders.

Each day the adults worked, stopping in time to milk the cows and feed the hogs and chickens. At night they sat after dusk, Sam reading his Bible by the light of a lamp after the children were in bed.

By Friday evening they had gotten three fourths of the crop into the barn, but the sky was beginning to cloud up again. The threatening rain held off until mid-morning on Saturday just as they were bringing in the first two loads of the day. Suddenly the rain came down in sheets and sent them racing to the barn. Sam opened the gate into the barnyard, and his wife drove the load under the overhang to keep it from getting wetter. Following at a fast trot with the second load, Andrew, his hair drenched and little rivulets of water dripping from his chin, spurred his team up the barn bank. The load swayed precipitously into the shelter of the mows. They would have to do some threshing before any more wheat could be brought in. There was scarcely room to unhitch the horses and lead them out when the rain stopped.

The wheat in the field needed time now to dry off again, and Andrew went home. Sunday was a day of rest from all work except caring for the animals and feeding the family. Field work was unthinkable. Simon Coblentz would not be finished with custom threshing until the oats were harvested. After that Andrew hoped to use the machinery at his brother, Sam's; and if it didn't rain too much, they might be able to save some of the wheat that was left in the field.

When Simon took the rig back to John Weaver's for the oats harvest, Andrew hoped for another chance to see Elizabeth. He watched the house for a glimpse of her. At noon when the men went in for dinner, he asked Sarah offhandedly where she was and found she was working for a Troyer family in Trail. He tried not to show his deep disappointment.

When the oats harvest was finished, Coblentz allowed Andrew to take the rig to Sam Yoder's. They threshed what wheat was left in the field, but much was wasted because the grains were over-ripened. Some of the oat crop was salvaged, but Sam Yoder had suffered a heavy loss.

The full impact of their personal loss would not be apparent until later when his children would be ostracized at school, his wife would be excluded from the quiltings the women held, and Sam would be barred from eating at his own mother's table by decree of the ministers. At night after the children were asleep, Emma cried softly into her pillow until Sam held her in his arms and comforted her.

Word got around to Bishop David Kauffman that Andrew had helped his brother with harvest, staying with them, eating at the same table. One evening Andrew sat relaxing outside on his mother's porch steps. The rough wooden boards were still warm from the afternoon sun. A cool breeze brought with it the sweet scent of honeysuckle that grew tangled on the picket fence. His mother sat rocking and knitting behind him. Occasionally she dozed and woke again, never dropping a stitch. His nieces came, and leaning on him one on each side, looked up admiringly as he played an old tune on his harmonica. "Believe me, if all those endearing young charms which I gaze on so fondly today, were to change by tomorrow and fleet in my arms," Catharina sang the words but could not remember them all. "No, the heart that has truly loved never forgets, but as truly loves on to the close," her voice broke off as horse hooves were heard approaching. "I wonder who comes," she said, gathering up her knitting and peering around the corner of the porch.

Bishop David Kauffman lighted from his buggy and tied his horse to the fence. He smiled as he heard the last strains of the familiar song, remembering his younger days. Greeting the little group, he lowered his ample body heavily onto the steps with a sigh. They talked of the weather, and Dave asked about Andrew's relatives in Indiana and other people he knew who had moved there.

Catharina, sensing their need for privacy, took her knitting indoors and lit the lamp. The little girls, finding the conversation tiring, ran off after fireflies, until their mother called them to come and wash their feet for bedtime.

"I guess harvesting is about over for this year," began the bishop pleasantly, taking out his pipe for a smoke, an indulgence he allowed himself on occasion.

"Yes, almost," agreed Andrew thinking of the wheat still stacked in Sam's barn waiting to be threshed.

The bishop tamped the tobacco, lit a match on the wooden step and drew leisurely on his pipe. After several unhurried puffs he began, "You know your brother, Sam, has decided to leave the church and join the 'house Amish' over in Berlin."

"Yes," Andrew answered tersely, "my mother recently informed me of that."

The bishop drew on his pipe and let his breath out in little puffs. "Of course we have had to put him under the ban. It's what the bishops of this area have decided, and it must be followed. You understand what that means, don't you?"

Andrew stared into the darkness as the bishop continued, "It's a hard thing, especially when it's your own brother, but if we let down the standards one place, they'll fall everywhere. I persuaded the brethren to overlook your association up to this time, you understand, but if you want to follow after the church, you have to promise to refrain from fellowshiping with your brother." He knocked the ashes from his pipe and prepared to leave. "You do want to follow after the church, still, don't you?"

Andrew felt the anger rise within him, but held his peace. "I'll have to think over it," he said at length, and the bishop drove off leaving him to contemplate his words.

A promise was not to be taken lightly. He loved his church and his people, but how could he turn his back on his brother?

CHAPTER IV

The little room under the eaves with its sloping ceiling was chilly, but the light from the kerosene lamp cast a glowing circle of warmth. Elizabeth shivered into her flannel nightgown, dancing from one foot to the other on the cold wooden floor. She knelt by the bed and quickly recited the German prayer her father had taught her when she was a little girl. Reaching under the straw mattress, she pulled out a book, turned up the flame and jumped under the quilts. She opened the book eager to begin the story. She closed her eyes and smelled its new, stiff pages.

A month ago, in mid-September, she had come to work as hired girl for Jacob and Anna Yoder who lived a mile and a half up over the hill from the Weavers, and past the schoolhouse. Anna was due to deliver her fourth child any time. She was having trouble with her legs, and Elizabeth was there to help with the chores and to help care for five-year-old Jacob, little David and baby Susie. Monday mornings she started early from home and walked to work in time to milk the cows for Jacob while he did the feeding and cleaned the stables.

It had been a golden autumn with blue skies. The orange pumpkins among the rows of corn shocks had glowed in the warm October sun. Elizabeth had expected that Andrew would be back before the summer was over, but she had not seen him. Many times she had relived the buggy ride with him in the storm, the tenderness in his eyes when he had looked at her. She had shared her feelings with no one but her sister, Sarah.

Now, as she lay in bed, the coverlets pulled up under her chin, her mind went back to that first Monday morning when she had walked up the hill to go to work at the Yoders'. The hike had made her warm, and she had shed her mantle and overcap. Stopping at the schoolhouse pump for a drink, she had encountered the new young teacher who had just tied his horse in the shed and came striding up to her with a tip of his hat. He offered to pump for her while she held the tin cup. He had reached out a soft, white hand and introduced himself, "Alfred Krantz. I'm the new teacher."

"Elizabeth Weaver," she had responded. "My brother and sister go here to school."

He had engaged her in conversation about the fine weather and other trivialities until she forgot her shyness in talking to a stranger.

Now it seemed she was running into Alfred every Monday when she walked to work or on Saturday evenings when she walked home. They had talked of many things. She learned that he rented a room in Walnut Creek, and that on Friday evenings he went home to Sugar Creek where he lived with his parents and sister. His father owned the drug store. She knew he was not one of them, the Amish. He wore store-bought suspenders and trousers; his hair was cut neatly around the ears in the current style, and his speech flowed fluently, self-assuredly.

One Monday morning when the grasses were crisp with frost and the brisk wind cut through her gray, wool shawl; she was invited to come into the school and warm herself. She held out her blue hands to the welcoming warmth of the great black stove that stood in the middle of the room. Alfred had come early to start the fire after the weekend. The air snapped with the sound of heat penetrating the walls and the wooden desks. She rubbed her hands and backed away from the glowing stove. Her eyes fell on the bookcase in the corner, and she walked over to peer in through the glass door. Alfred took the key from his drawer, and with two quick steps he was at her side unlocking the door.

Elizabeth drew in her breath at sight of the rows of colorful books. She had read most of the textbooks in the top of her father's cherry desk: *Pilgrim's Progress, McGuffey's Eclectic Readers.* She had looked at the prints in the big German Bible that had been her great-grandfather's. Then there were several copies of *Die Ausbund*, the song book which they took to Sunday meetings. Grandmother Veronica Miller had a large, heavy book called *Martyr's Mirror* which she had let Elizabeth look at as a child. The engravings had fascinated her as Grandmother related stories of the brave people of long ago who had suffered and died rather than give up their faith. Her access to literature had been meager. The books in Alfred's bookcase with their bright covers begged her to read them. On the middle shelf was a row of newer books, unscuffed, unread. Alfred saw her hungry stare and pulled out *Little Women*. For several minutes they stood with heads bent over the book, he turning the pages with a smooth, manicured hand.

"You enjoy reading, don't you?" He shoved the book into her hands. "Here." She laid a finger on it pensively. "Take it and keep it as long as you like. When you are finished you can choose another."

Her blue eyes twinkled with excitement, and the round lips parted to speak, but no words came out. She hoped it was all right to take it. Slowly she slid it into her gray cloth bag between her flannel gown and her extra apron. He saw the thanks in her eyes as she pulled on her black, quilted cap. "I really must be going," she said.

Every week the books she chose opened up new vistas to her eager imagination. As she pushed the heavy irons over Jacob's blue cotton shirts, she thought of Heidi and her grandfather in faraway Switzerland. Washing up the milking utensils in the mornings, she imagined Sir Walter Scott's beautiful Rowena standing in the castle of King Richard. Now as she lay thinking, her thoughts came back to the book in her hand. Tom was going to take Becky's punishment; she wanted to read on and on until the book was finished. But Anna would wonder, if she saw her light still on. Jacob could be heard shaking the grate and putting on more coal to bank the fire. Reluctantly she put the book back into its hiding place. Cupping her hand over the glass chimney of the lamp, she turned the flame low and blew it out with a quick little puff, then lay down and fell asleep.

Some hours later, Elizabeth awoke with a start. She lay still, listening. It was not yet time to rise. Presently she heard men's voices coming toward the house, and suddenly she knew; Jacob had brought the doctor. Anna's time had come. Jumping out of bed, Elizabeth dressed quickly in the dark and went downstairs where Anna lay on the bed in the dim light of a kerosene lamp, exhausted from the labor pangs that had receded

let up for the moment. Beads of sweat shone on her forehead.

Jacob had replenished the fires before he left, and kettles of water bubbled on the kitchen stove. One of the children wailed in sleep in the little room adjacent to the bedroom. Elizabeth went to comfort him, pulling the covers up around his ears, so he would not hear his mother crying out as the pain began again. She gathered the old sheets which Anna had kept ready, and brought hot water at the doctor's instruction.

Jacob sat in the kitchen, his head bowed down on his chest, helplessly agonizing as husbands have for millennia. He rose startled as the portly, bespectacled Doctor Zahner came out of the bedroom. "It will be very soon," the doctor said, pulling his gold watch from his vest pocket and disappearing again to sit by the bed and wait, dozing. The husband paced between door and table, a look of feeble anguish on his bearded face as the sound of pain pierced through the walls again. For a few tense minutes all was utterly quiet. Somewhere a rooster crowed. Then there came the soft, unsteady cry of a newborn, and the smell of blood as the doctor pushed through the door carrying a small whimpering bundle and laid it in Jacob's arms. "A little girl," he announced, going back to collect his bag of instruments.

The father smiled proudly at his newborn daughter and handing her to Elizabeth, he took a dollar from a drawer high up in the cupboard to pay the doctor. Then he went to his wife's side to soothe her, his rough hands gently stroking her hair until she fell into sleep.

Elizabeth bathed the squalling baby with practiced hands, wrapped her in soft, clean flannel and laid her, sleeping, beside Anna. She tidied the room and set the soiled cloths to soak in a tub of salt water in the wash house. She paused at the bedroom door.

"You might just as well sleep for a little while before it's time to do chores," Jacob suggested kindly.

"All right. Knock on the stove pipe when it's time, and I'll feed the cows and do the milking. You stay with Anna."

The baby whimpered and turned its head from side to side in search of nourishment. Anna cradled it in the crook of her arm and guided its mouth to her bulging breast. Elizabeth went upstairs and flung herself fully clothed on her cot to sleep until daylight came, and a new day of work began. Anna stayed in bed for nine days as was the custom for new mothers. It was a good time for a baby to be born; the heavy summer work was over. There was still some corn to husk, but the butchering would not begin until the weather turned colder. Jacob was able to do the chores and keep the older children with him when he worked around the barn.

Elizabeth's days were so filled with extra laundry, wiping noses, cooking and cleaning, that at night she went to bed exhausted, not able to keep her eyes open to read. She would not be able to go home at the end of the week. On Friday afternoon, when Susie and David were down for a nap, Elizabeth took little Jacob by the hand, and they walked to the school. It was almost dismissal time. Alfred caught sight of her coming down the road. Her soft knock turned all heads toward the door as Alfred invited her to step inside with, "What a pleasant surprise!"

"I can't stay long," she answered. "The Yoders have a new little one, and Anna will need me if the children wake up. I want to talk to Joseph and Annie."

Alfred hoped she had not only come to talk to her brother and sister. He heard her explain to them, "Tell Mem I won't be coming home this evening. Jacobs have a new little one, and I have to stay and help them over Sunday." Though she spoke in the Pennsylvania German dialect, the teacher could understand the message.

The children were dismissed with much jostling and slamming of books. They sat quietly at their desks until Alfred gave the signal. Then they filed out by rows, grabbing jackets and lunch buckets and giving the teacher a polite handshake as they left. "I hope you each have a pleasant Sabbath," he said formally as they bounded away. The boys whooped and shouted after each other scattering toward their homes. The girls walked more demurely in little groups. Elizabeth waved to her brother and sister and turned to go, little Jacob still gripping her hand, his eyes wide in wonder at this strange, new world he had entered.

"Does that mean I won't see you on Monday morning?" Alfred queried with a note of disappointment.

"I guess it does," she replied dryly.

"You may choose another book now if you like."

"I haven't had time to finish the last one."

"Tom Sawyer," he murmured. "Did you find it exciting?"

"Oh, yes, very much. But the work has been more since the little one came. There is not much time for reading. Perhaps there will be time on Sunday."

He nodded understandingly. "Why don't you slip over after school on Monday in case Joseph and Anna have a message for you from home. You could get another book then."

"I'll see, and thank you," she smiled without promising. "Good-bye." She hurried away, her small charge running to keep up. With a certain degree of alarm, she had noted in Alfred's contacts a more than casual interest in her, but she was careful not to encourage him. There could be no harm in using the books he lent her. They were a great source of pleasure to her, taking her out of the humdrum of her everyday duties.

Elizabeth longed for the rough and tumble play of Peter and Benjamin, the joking and laughing around the family table. Her grandfather, Peter Miller, encouraged many family gatherings when uncles, aunts and cousins sat down at a feast together. Sometimes in the fall the men hunted, and occasionally the women took a trip to Strasburg to shop in the big department store. They visited in each others' homes on Sundays and stood by in times of sorrow or need. While there was always much work to be done, it was seasoned with jollity and humor.

Uncle Johnny was a great favorite when he came home from his excursions to the West. Grandmother Veronica exchanged letters with him relating the neighborhood gossip and the family activities. His last note, from South Dakota, had talked of coming home "if it gives *Hochzeit*" a reference to Sarah's pending nuptials. Ten years Elizabeth's senior, he had not married as yet, and much of what he did was a mystery to her, but she knew he would come loaded with gifts and a bag of new tricks to amaze and startle, and there would be times of merriment.

Monday afternoon found Elizabeth at the schoolhouse door again just as the children dispersed homeward. Alfred in his trim, brown suit watched as Joseph delivered his message to her. "Mem said some people, Nolts, in

Sugar Creek want you to work for them when you are done at Jake's."

Elizabeth nodded assent, her hopes dashed of spending time at home with her family. It was a young girl's duty, when she wasn't needed at home, to hire out as maid to help supplement the family income and lay aside something for the time when she married. "Tell the folks I'll be home on Friday evening, but then Anna wants me another week." Joseph waved good-bye and ran to catch up with his friends, swinging his empty lunch pail over his head.

Alfred slipped the copy of *Tom Sawyer* into its place and held the bookcase door open for Elizabeth to browse through the colorful volumes.

"So you'll be working in Sugar Creek?" he began.

"It sounds that way," she replied gravely. "For two weeks."

"If you need a way over, you're welcome to ride with me when I go home for the weekend."

"My brother, Peter, will be driving me over Sunday afternoon, but thank you."

"My sister and I often go to Beach City and take the trolley in to Canton for the day. It's great sport," he said, searching her face. "I'm sure you and Alice would get on capitally. Have you ever been there?"

"No, I haven't, but Peter and our cousin, Danny Miller, took the trolley with a group of young folks once this summer."

"I'm sure they had a splendid time. Did Peter tell you about the nickelodeons and the vaudeville shows?"

She shook her head. She had never heard of either, and her curiosity was piqued.

She wondered that her brother had never mentioned them. It sounded exciting.

"They have stories on moving pictures, and in the summer you can ride the Ferris wheel. My sister and I think it's smashing fun. I hope you'll come with us," he urged.

"I'll see," she smiled.

Emboldened by her fascination, he would have regaled her further with descriptions of the flickering flicks and the band concerts, but she had to go back to her duties. He watched her go, a volume of *Call of the Wild* tucked under her arm and little Jacob skipping beside her; and Alfred thought with anticipation of the prospects ahead.

That night Elizabeth's dreams were jumbled with trolley rides and strangers' faces. The only familiar face was Andrew's, and always there seemed to be obstacles between them.

CHAPTER V

Elizabeth had almost exhausted Alfred's stock of books by the time she finished work at the Yoders', but when she went to Sugar Creek to work for several weeks as housemaid to Mrs. Nolt, she had a copy of Jane Austin's *Pride and Prejudice* in her bag of clothes. Peter drove her down in the top buggy on Sunday. It was a sunny afternoon, the hills were still colorful with crimson and gold against the blue sky, and the fallen leaves splashed the ground with radiant color. The air was still and warm in the valleys, and Peter had rolled up his shirtsleeves. Elizabeth took off her bonnet and shawl. She wished the pleasant ride wouldn't have to end and tried not to think about breaking in at a new place and learning the new ways of strangers.

What would it be like? Would Alfred come over to see her as he had said he intended? His increasing attentiveness concerned her. She thoroughly enjoyed the books he lent her, but did he expect something in return? Did he have feelings for her that she could not reciprocate? She certainly did not want to encourage his interest in her.

She glanced at Peter lounging easily in the seat, whistling a tuneless song and letting the horse pick its own way on the narrow road that rambled through woods, over streams and up and down the hills. Little clouds of dust rose from the hooves as the horse ambled along. Elizabeth was a year and a half younger than her brother, but perhaps because he was a boy, he seemed younger than his age. He never appeared to have a worry in the world.

"What did you do the day you rode the trolley into town?" she asked abruptly.

Peter sat up, his face coming to life. "Didn't I ever tell you about it? I guess you were working away from home at the time." He studied the back of his hand. "Well, we rode the Ferris Wheel. That was great fun!"

"Wasn't it frightening?" she asked.

"Naw. I and Danny stayed on it for a half hour anyhow. Joe got nervous at the top and couldn't wait to get off." They laughed. "You should have been there to hearten him," Peter teased, though he knew she didn't like Joe. Elizabeth scowled at him.

"There's a park where you get off the trolley," Peter continued. "Has lots of interesting things to see, new things. They even had a machine that washes dishes!"

"Oh, my!" She couldn't imagine how that could be.

"There was also a wild west show, Indians and cowboys; and some went in to see a flick."

"Did you, too, Peter?"

"No, but Danny did."

"What did Uncle Dan and Aunt Katie say about that?"

"He never told them. Said, 'what they don't know won't hurt 'em'," Peter chuckled.

They came to a place where the road crossed a stream. Peter let the reins slack so the horse could drink and rest a bit.

"The teacher wants me to go with him and his sister to Canton on the trolley one Saturday," Elizabeth confided, giving her brother a sidelong glance. "Do you think I should?"

"Sure, why not?" Peter clicked his tongue to the horse and slapped the reins. The carriage wobbled, its steel rims grinding on the stony stream bed. He looked askance at his sister. "Do you fancy the teacher?"

Elizabeth turned her head in surprise, "No, of course not! Not that way. Why do you ask?"

"I saw you get out of his buggy a couple times when you came home from Jake Yoders'."

"I was walking home, and Alfred came along and offered me a ride. I figured I might as well. I was glad for a chance to sit down. Besides, I didn't want to be rude. He's been nice to me."

"He's been nice to you? How?" His eyes searched her face.

Realizing she had said more than she had planned, Elizabeth knew she had to tell her brother about her casual encounters with the teacher. She could trust him with her secret. "Alfred has been lending me books to read since I started working at Yoders'. They're good books, and it makes the time go faster," she confided.

Peter was contemplative. "There's nothing wrong with that," he answered. After a moment he added, "Wasn't it a little late for *Alfred*," giving the name emphasis, "to be going home all the way to Sugar Creek? Are you sure he didn't plan it that way?" Peter teased, but seeing the distressed look that came over her face, he said no more about it.

It was four o'clock when they stopped at Nolts' door. Peter carried his sister's things up onto the porch and said good-bye. She waved to him until the buggy turned the corner and was out of sight. Elizabeth noted the wide veranda with its white railings and pillars. The house was a big Victorian one with many rooms, lace curtains on the windows and carpets on the stairs. Elizabeth would be helping with the fall house cleaning.

The stairs creaked under Mrs. Nolt's generous frame as she showed her hired girl to the bedroom she would occupy. In the kitchen she lit the gas lamp and put on a kettle for tea, her husband joining them at the table. She chatted pleasantly, stirring her tea. "I like to have my house all cleaned by this time in the fall, but I was feeling poorly the last while and didn't have any push. I'm so glad for your help. It was a lucky thing that I ran into your mother in the dry goods store one day. It's so hard to find help," she rattled on. "If it's sunny again tomorrow, we'll hang the blankets out to air and wash and stretch the curtains. We eat supper at about half past five, then after the dishes are done, you can lay out the breakfast things and have the rest of the evening to yourself. Saturday and Sunday you can have off, too, if you want to go home, though you're welcome to stay. Charles, call the boys to come in," she added to her husband without pausing.

Just as her husband stood up there was a tapping on the door, and as he swung it open, there stood Alfred looking casual in his gray sweater and knickers. His sister, Alice, peered over his shoulder, the feather on her hat bobbing. Alfred would be going back to work in the early morning and so had lost no time in coming over to arrange for Elizabeth to spend the next weekend with them. Alice, his accomplice in carrying out his plans, looked smart in a long, full skirt and a lacy white shirt waist that was the latest fashion.

"We were just out for a ride and thought we'd see if you had gotten here." Smiling at Elizabeth, he introduced the girls.

"Charmed, I'm sure," Alice responded. Her eyes traveled up and down over Elizabeth's petite figure making a mental evaluation according to her own criteria. *How drab and quaint. What does he see in her? Still she might have possibilities.* She felt a twinge of envy at the naturally curly hair, the creamy complexion and the trim waistline. The girl had a natural beauty that with Alice's practiced hand could be stunning. She only needed a little dressing up. Alice was starting to take a liking to her.

When Alfred and his sister left, the plans had all been laid out. They would take the trolley early on Saturday morning. Elizabeth wished she could go home on Friday evening. She wished she could be with Andy again.

Lucy Nolt was pleased with her hired girl who learned to stretch the lace curtains to her exacting satisfaction. Elizabeth beat the rugs as they hung on the line until there was not a whit of dust left in them. Many of these tasks had never been required of her in the Amish homes where the floors were bare and the furnishings simple.

On Friday evening Alice came by to pick her up in the carriage. They stopped at her father's drug store for a quick refreshment at the soda fountain. Sitting on a tall bar stool, Elizabeth watched fascinated at the sparkling water flowing from the shiny spigot. The bubbly drink stung her nose a little at first.

She felt pampered at dinner later as they were served by the Irish maid, but she found it difficult to join in the conversation. The women's talk was of clothes and vacations at the seaside; the men's of stocks, prices and new inventions.

"Your mother and I were looking to buy an automobile by spring," Mr. Krantz was saying.

"Swell," said Alice, suddenly becoming interested in the men's conversation.

"What kind?" from Alfred.

"We both liked the Packard we looked at. It's good for driving in the city."

"So stylish, too," put in Mrs. Krantz.

"However, on country roads they say the little Ford is better. You know how muddy the roads can get," stated Mr. Krantz.

"Will you be here for dinner tomorrow evening?" Mrs. Krantz interrupted.

"No, probably not," Alfred answered. "We'll eat in a restaurant before we come home."

"I'll tell the cook, then," said Mrs. Krantz rising.

They all retired to the parlor, Mr. Krantz behind the paper with his pipe. His wife sat down at the organ but was interrupted by Alice from time to time with remarks about what women were wearing according to *Ladies Home Journal*. Alfred rescued Elizabeth with their stereoscopic slides, and soon she felt at ease marveling at the realistic pictures of nature and laughing with him at the funny antics of the comic actors who played out a slapstick story.

In her bedroom the next morning, Alice selected several of her dresses and held them up to her guest who reluctantly chose a simple dark green gingham that Alice said had gotten too tight for her. It had a high, lace collar, leg-o-mutton sleeves and a row of tiny buttons down the back. "You look simply smashing!" Alice pronounced. "I have just the hat to go with it." She produced a straw with a wide ribbon to match the dress.

Elizabeth felt slightly uncomfortable in such finery. The only hats she had ever worn were the plain straw hats that kept the sun out of her face when working in garden or field. Her help was solicited to lace up the corset which Alice put on in an attempt at an hourglass figure.

"Tighter, tighter!" Alice commanded holding on to the bedpost as Elizabeth obediently pulled at the laces until they seemed to her torturously taut. After that Alice walked around stiffly, her breath going in and out in shallow gasps.

Elizabeth went downstairs leaving Alice to finish arranging her hair. Standing in Mr. Krantz's library, she scanned the dull, leather-bound volumes. Undetected, Alfred walked up behind her, startling her with his touch.

"My little bookworm! Looking for books. If I weren't here to save you, you would stay in a corner and read all day."

She did not find his casual manner agreeable. *If only he knew how much I really would prefer doing that,* she thought, pulling away politely.

"Have you read any of Jane Austin?" Alfred asked.

"I've only finished the first five chapters," she responded. "I think I will really enjoy that book."

"You're not going to find anything very interesting here among these pharmaceutical books. Let's get going. Where's Alice?"

But Alice was just then descending the stairs, pouting and looking a little pudgy. Her attempt at a willowy silhouette had been reluctantly abandoned. "I'm not going!" she declared.

"Of course you're going. Billy would be terribly disappointed," said her brother.

"But I look awful! Just matronly," she insisted.

"You look splendid, Sis! Really you do. It won't be any fun without you." With these words he cajoled her into going.

Alfred's friend, Billy, had been invited to be Alice's escort and was at the trolley station when they arrived.

Alfred doted on Elizabeth, plying her with ice creams and candies, not aware that his possessiveness was only making her feel more and more uncomfortable. She couldn't remember what had come over her to make her agree to this outing. The rides that would have been a lark with her brother and his friends made her nauseated. She wished the day would end. She wanted to take off this finery and curl up on her bed with a good book.

"Anybody hungry?" Let's get a bite," suggested Alfred pulling Elizabeth toward the door of a dairy bar.

At that moment she spotted down the midway two wiry young men wearing straight, blue denims with homemade suspenders and wide-

55

brimmed hats. She sucked in her breath as they looked in her direction for an instant. It was Joe and one of the Burkholder boys. They evidently hadn't recognized her, and she ducked willingly into the shop with Alfred. Billy, with Alice giggling beside him, followed them into a booth. If Joe had seen her, the news would be gossiped all over by Sunday that Isaac John's Lizzie was seen with the teacher at the amusement park. She had a sudden impulse to let Joe take her home, but quickly put the thought aside, stirring her soda listlessly.

"Penny for your thoughts," said Alice.

Elizabeth gave her a weak smile. "I guess I'm just getting a little tired."

"Oh, yes, you're a country girl and probably used to going to bed with the chickens," Alice laughed loudly. She had noted all day with mounting chagrin the roving glances that Elizabeth drew from the young chaps.

Alfred, seeing his friend's embarrassment, broke in, "I'm getting tired myself. Some of us work during the week, you know." He took Elizabeth's elbow and steered her toward the door.

Glowering, Alice grabbed Billy's hand and strutted off. "Let's go see a flick," she suggested, and the others obediently followed. Consequently, Elizabeth found herself between Alfred and Alice watching *The Great Train Robbery*. She felt pangs of guilt knowing her folks would not approve, nonetheless there was really nothing she could do and wanting to be a congenial companion, she let herself get caught up in the story and delighted in the fun.

When Alfred dropped her off at the Nolts', he held both of her hands, and looking into her eyes, queried, "Can we do it again soon? Maybe we could go dancing."

Seeing her answer in her averted eyes as she drew her hands from his, he quickly suggested, "Let's go to the library next Saturday and browse, find some good books to read."

Her eyes lit up. "I would like that," she answered.

"We'll eat lunch at the cafe and then go to my house and read all afternoon," he proposed with anticipation.

"Won't you have lessons to grade?" she questioned, half teasing. She felt more comfortable with him when Alice was not there.

"I'll work late every night and give the scholars easy assignments," he answered her challenge grinning.

The weather turned bitterly cold and brought icicles on the eaves, and by week's end there was a thick layer of ice on the ponds and streams. On Saturday afternoon, each with an armload of books, the pair settled around the stove in the parlor to indulge themselves in the pastime they both relished.

"Why don't we read a book aloud together, "Alfred recommended. "We'll take turns reading and then talk about what we've read." So after scanning the novels, they agreed on *The Adventures of Huckleberry Finn.* Taking turns reading, they became so engrossed in Huck's escapades that the hours flew by unregarded. Every detail of the story was so exciting that when Alice and Mr. and Mrs. Krantz came home from shopping and other pursuits in late afternoon, they found the two completely preoccupied with their story. Huck and Jim had just come across a gang of thieves when the two young people had to abandon them.

"How often have I told you not to read in the dark?" Mrs. Krantz chided her son, stepping across the room to light the big gas lamp.

Alice caught Elizabeth's hand and pulled her to the stairs. "I want to show you the stunning pair of shoes I bought," she said breezily.

The quiet afternoon was over, but Elizabeth was persuaded into staying overnight. She had truly enjoyed the day in Alfred's company. He had graciously prevailed on her to take the book which they hadn't finished, and she read it late into the night.

The next day everyone got into their finery and rode to church in the big surrey. After dinner Elizabeth slipped into the kitchen and proceeded washing the dinner plates. Bridget, the maid, objected, "You must no' soil your Sunday clothes, lass. It's me job, and I'll be doin' it."

"But I'm used to doing dishes. It would make me feel at home."

"Thank you, lass, but you're our guest and I'll 'ave none of it," Bridget insisted.

"If it makes her feel at home, by all means let her help," said Alfred who had stuck his head through the doorway and had heard their conversation. "Do you want to wash or dry?" he asked Elizabeth.

"I can do either or both, but I don't know about you," she answered laughing.

"Here's an apron for ye then," said Bridget tossing her one and joining in the fun. Elizabeth caught it and slipped it playfully over Alfred's head. He feigned resistance to the feminine garment, but obediently let her tie it behind him.

It was like being with her brother, Peter, the splashing and bantering and laughing. When they were finished, Alfred suggested, "How about going down to the mill pond for some skating? Billy said it froze thick enough this week and there's no snow on it, so it should be good. Alice has a pair of skates she never uses," he added before she could object.

"But I've only skated a few times, and I'll do nothing but fall down," she protested.

"That's where I come in," he said chivalrously. "I will teach you and make sure you stay upright, and soon you'll be dazzling all the spectators."

The air was crisp but still. The sun shining from the naked sky made the ice glisten. Children and youths glided to and fro filling the atmosphere with merriment. Elizabeth and Alfred skated around and around the pond, she clinging to his arm, he steadying and guiding her, until at last their strides became rhythmic and graceful. Though there were other young folks on the ice, Alfred made sure none of the striplings got a chance to conduct her around the ring. Before the afternoon was over he had taught her to negotiate a respectable figure eight. He was very proud, but they would both pay for their fun with stiff muscles next day.

At dusk the two friends walked back to the Krantz home, rosy and tingling from the cold, fresh air. They gulped the warm soup Bridget had waiting. They had both had a marvelously good time and hated to see it end. Having gotten over her reserve, Elizabeth had found Alfred to be a perfect gentleman and a stimulating companion. The "weekend", as Alice liked to call it, had truly been fun. He had never given any hint of wanting her for more than a good friend.

"Well, I'd best be getting on back to the Nolts'," said Elizabeth.

"You mean to say all good things must come to an end?" answered

Alfred, unable to hide his disappointment. "I wish you didn't have to go just yet, but if you must, I'll go and bring the carriage around."

"I've really had a wonderful time, but tomorrow it's back to work for both of us."

"You really are quite good on the ice already," Alfred remarked as they rode across town in his buggy. "What do you say we try it again, say, Friday evening?"

"This is my last week at the Nolts'," she declared. "My sister will be getting married in a few weeks, and there are mountains of work to be done. But thank you for the invitation," she added noting his let down expression.

"You could ride back with me on Sunday afternoon if you like," he tried again.

"Peter is coming to fetch me on Friday evening," she answered. Then remembering the library books, she asked, "What shall I do about the books?"

"Oh, keep them and read them," he exclaimed, hopeful at the prospect of future contacts with her. "I will stop by and pick them up some evening," he said, thinking of the supply he could keep coming and going thus providing him a legitimate alibi for stopping to see her regularly.

Elizabeth wondered what her parents would think about the teacher stopping by to bring her books. She was sure her mother would consider it trifling foolishness, if nothing more; she found her satisfaction in productive work and found little need for meaningless diversions. But Elizabeth would have to cross that bridge when she got to it. She waved goodby to Alfred and went in.

Riding home with Peter the following Friday afternoon, they chatted about butchering hogs, husking the last of the corn, and preparing for Sarah's wedding. The minute the horse and buggy were heard at the gate, Annie came racing out excitedly, a shawl pulled askew over her head, to greet her sister with, "Uncle Johnny's coming home! Mummy got a letter today. He was in Californy or some place like that."

CHAPTER VI

Elizabeth was glad to be home where the furnishings and the people alike were simple and unpretentious. People said what they meant and meant what they said. There was no incentive to put on airs. Around the supper table, her brothers' good-natured banter was all the amusement they needed. Her parents' talk of fundamental things like the price they got for eggs and butter, of cheese making and butchering, of weddings and new babies made the remembered conversations between Alice and her mother seem laughingly trivial. *Which would look better, the flat lace or the ruffle? I must have one of those. They're all the go now!*

The first cornmeal mush from the fall crop tasted delectable; and more satisfying than the crumpets she'd been served at breakfast was the apple butter on Mem's homemade bread. No one indulged in idleness in the Weaver household. After work there was time for play. Each had his or her tasks to do, and if anyone didn't come to the table ravenously hungry, it was regarded as a sign that they were ill.

A festive spirit governed the atmosphere tonight with talk of the wedding and Uncle Johnny's coming. The prayer said, everyone dipped hungrily into their steaming bowls of mush and milk. When the edge was off their appetites, the conversation began to flow again.

"Remember when Uncle Johnny pinned the pig's tail on Uncle Henry's behind and he went to meeting with it on?" The children burst into laughter.

"Yah, and remember when he convinced Joe Mast that a horse hair would turn into a snake if you put it in water?" someone began.

"Ha, he put some water on the hair on the table and told Joe to watch very closely," someone else took up the story. "And when Joe had his nose down watching closely, Johnny went *slap* on the table and splashed water all over Joe's face." The room exploded with shrieks of laughter and knee slapping.

"Children, children," John cautioned sternly, temporarily subduing them.

"Hopefully Johnny has grown up a little since then," Susanna asserted about her younger brother. "Uncle Henry never will, but you boys had better be good!"

They all looked forward to Johnny's homecomings from roaming the West with stories of his escapades and his bag of tricks. His letter had said he would start home as soon as the apple crop was harvested. He would be there for Sarah's wedding.

John signaled for bowed heads and a moment of silence that accompanied the end of every meal. The prayer over, there was a scurry of chairs as the younger girls fell to clearing the table. Elizabeth drew a pan of hot water from the stove reservoir, while the boys grabbed their overshoes and caps and headed outside to finish their chores of putting down hay for the livestock and cleaning stables.

The chatter about Uncle Johnny's tricks continued with much snickering. Benjamin confided in Peter, "I hope he hasn't gotten all growed up and stiff and sober."

"Don't worry, Benj," Peter reassured him, "Uncle Johnny will always be Uncle Johnny. Age will never change him." Laughing, he added, "Remember when he put that nest of baby mice in Uncle Henry's coat pocket?"

Leaning on their pitchforks, the boys roared with laughter. "Uncle Henry was so mad. He likes to do pranks on other people, but he can't take it when they get him back."

"I wonder what Johnny has planned for him this time." They chuckled at the prospect of seeing the favorite butt of Johnny's pranks being out-tricked.

Uncle Henry's fat little wife, Lizzie, was Grandmother Veronica's younger sister and it would have been hard to conceive of anyone more different from her than her namesake, Elizabeth. Spoiled and idle as a child, she had never learned industriousness which is so typical of Amish people. When she and Henry were married, they were nearing middle age and never had any children. She always carried peppermints in her pockets to suck on and to treat her grand-nephews and nieces. They lived forty miles northeast of the Walnut Creek community so couldn't come often, but when they came, it was for an extended stay of weeks, visiting for several days with each relative in the environs. Never wanting to miss any of the celebrating, they were expected to make their appearance soon.

The days were getting shorter and colder. The last of the corn was shocked. Some of it would be husked later in the barn when the young people got together for a husking bee on a winter night.

One evening in mid-November Uncle Johnny arrived, his hat at a rakish angle as he walked jauntily down the lane singing. Grandfather Peter had picked him up at the train station. He was eagerly received by all the younger set. There was an added note of merriment in the air whenever Johnny was about, and the elders were glad for the extra hand at butchering.

Next day, as soon as the morning chores were done and before the sun was up, the butchering began. Four fat hogs were killed and hung on wooden trivets where an array of people in shawls and heavy woolens set about scraping the bristles off with sharp knives. The bellies were gutted, letting the steaming entrails flow out.

Soon eight hams were ready to be salted down and hung in the smokehouse where they would be cured for many weeks. Some of the meat was cured in crocks filled with brine. The head meat was cooked and made into sausage. The liver, cooked along with scraps of meat became liverwurst to be fried and eaten with corn mush throughout the winter. There would be plenty of meat for the wedding feast, and tonight there would be sweetbreads for supper. The women cleaned the intestines for sausage casings, scraping them carefully, so they would have fewer holes but be as thin as crepe de chine. The next day Elizabeth cranked the sausage stuffer while Johnny deftly guided the casings singing a hilarious tune he had learned in the West.

The butchering done, the women set to work scrubbing and dusting the house from attic to cellar. The bare wooden floors were rubbed with sandstone until they were smooth and white. Bedding was hung on the porch to air, and the windows were washed inside and out. Instead of the old, faded curtains, new blue ones were sewn and hung. Stoves were blackened and polished. Backhouse, stables and sheds were cleaned and limed. The men brought benches to the shed ready to be set up in the house the day before the wedding. There was a flurry of new dresses, caps and shirts.

Peter and Benjamin drove to and fro throughout the countryside inviting friends and neighbors for a day of feasting and frolic. Veronica sent a note to her girlhood chum, Catharina, and her son, Andrew, to join them for the wedding festivities.

Elizabeth's nineteenth birthday was almost forgotten in the bustle. Her mother remembered to bake a cake, and Sarah wrote "Lizzie" on top with frosting. After supper the boys and Uncle Johnny, at a prearranged signal, stood up, and grabbing her chair at the four corners, hoisted her to the ceiling with much protest and screaming from Elizabeth. Then they all took turns pulling her ears and spanking her nineteen times. Uncle Johnny teased her, "Sweet nineteen and never been kissed?"

The late fall and winter season was the time for *Hochzeit*. The fall work was finished, some of the butchering done; and with all the food to prepare ahead for the days of feasting, cold weather was welcome to help in preserving the meats, puddings and pastries.

Sarah's marriage to John Herschberger was set for Thursday of the second week in December. Two weeks before, the bans were published in the Sunday meeting. Sarah had demurely slipped out unnoticed before Bishop Eli made the announcement.

Uncle Henry and Aunt Lizzie arrived a week ahead, conspicuously in a mood for feasting and jollity. Uncle Henry's reputation of love for boisterous humor did not disappoint his nephews. His round, little wife largely disregarded his boyish activities, preferring time spent in friendly gossip with the women and enjoying the culinary delights she tasted without much urging. Her activity consisted largely of walking from couch to table and back again. Having been coddled as a child, she was not given to offering a hand at household chores.

The family had tolerated Henry's behavior for ten years now and had learned to be cautious of thumbs pushed into the butter as it was passed, of chairs pulled out just as one got ready to sit down or of a foot thrust out as one walked by. Johnny and Henry watched each other warily out of the corners of their eyes. Henry had a score to settle, and he watched for an opportunity. Though the young nephews assumed an air of nonchalance, they were extremely interested in the contest that was sure to be waged in the coming days and were placing their bets on Johnny. They didn't have long to wait.

By Thursday, the eve of the wedding the house was already filling with people, young people who traditionally came to celebrate with the engaged couple and people who had traveled a distance and would stay several nights. The adults and the younger children had retired to the "*däddy* house" leaving the young people to entertain themselves alone.

It was a chilly night; a little snow had fallen. The young men pulled their chairs close around the stove while the girls huddled in little groups on the fringes, listening to their talk. Uncle Johnny, as usual, was the center of attention, enrapturing his audience with tales of the wild West, stories of Indians and buffaloes he had seen from the train, of roping cattle and harvesting wheat. With so many attentive eyes turned on him, he was not above a little embellishment here and there. Uncle Henry had naively chosen to stay behind with the youths. Not wanting to miss a bit of the fun, he settled himself in a chair by the stove adding his remarks from time to time and taking particular enjoyment in heckling the young star of the evening. He had a native insensitivity that made him impervious to the disdain with which his intrusion was regarded, and so he pressed on boldly trying to humiliate the younger, quicker-witted Johnny.

"Are you sure the bear you saw wasn't one of those Western cows? Hah, hah, hah!" Henry blared. Johnny took no note of him.

"You should have married one of those Indian squaws to keep you warm at night, or wouldn't they have you?"

Johnny knew he could afford to be patient. Finally he turned to Henry with a proposal. "I hear you're pretty good at arm wrestling!"

Easily flattered, Henry's face lit up imagining himself to be much more virile than he was seen by others. He willingly forgot the truth that his

65

arms had gotten soft and flabby.

"If you can beat me, I'll buy you a keg of beer," Johnny baited his victim.

They faced each other across a wooden table and grasped hands. Feigning a tremendous struggle, Johnny eventually let Henry push his arm down onto the table and claim victory. "All right," said Johnny," you've won fair and square. Hitch up your horse and I'll meet you down at the tavern."

"Oh, no," bawled Henry smugly, "you're not playing that trick on me! I wasn't born yesterday." Pleased with himself, he looked around at the group for approval.

"If that's the way you want it, I'll go ahead. It pains me that my own uncle doesn't trust my word." Johnny winked slyly at Peter who grinned from ear to ear wondering what Uncle Johnny was up to. "Come on, boys, you'll be our witnesses," said Johnny holding up a roll of bills.

Henry sat festively at the bar while Johnny paid for several drinks, and ordered a five-gallon barrel to be sent with Henry when he was finished emptying the row of beer glasses before him. With a tip of his hat, Johnny was out the door followed by his buddies, who thought it was a cunning trick to get Henry out of their hair so they could enjoy the rest of the evening without his annoying presence.

But Johnny was not finished with his plan. With Ben stationed outside the door to make sure Henry was busy, Johnny went out to where the horses were tied and found his uncle's horse and buggy. He posted Joe at the horse's head to keep him calm and, with Peter holding a lantern, set to work removing the wheels one at a time while the other boys held up the buggy. The smaller front wheels were switched to the back and the larger back wheels to the front.

By the time Henry came out slightly tipsy, carrying his barrel, the boys had gone home. A thin covering of snow had obliterated their footprints. Henry felt something very strange in the tilt of the carriage and the way the keg kept wanting to roll out, but being in a jovial mood, he decided it was nothing. Feeling things were not right, Barney, the horse, stopped dead in his tracks and refused to budge, though Henry shouted curses at him and flung the whip at his back finding his aim to be very poor. After some minutes, he decided to get out and try to persuade the horse to get started. Slipping on the slanting step, he rolled into the snow and noticed the wheels were all wrong. *Had he been going backwards? No!* More sober now, he evaluated the situation. "I mighta' known. This is one of Johnny's tricks!" he said under his breath. He groveled on the snowy road trying to get his footing, then stood up angrily shouting epithets into the wind. The frightened Barney suddenly bolted and took off down the road at great speed, the buggy flying behind him, leaving Henry shaking his fist at the unpleasant predicament in which he found himself.

The horse would have passed by Weavers', but the young culprits, standing watch to see what would become of their prank, caught and unhitched him, putting him and the buggy safely into the barn. Having no intention of leaving his barrel behind, Henry rolled it and carried it up and down the hills until at last he arrived at Peter and Veronica's gate. He trudged dejectedly in and up the stairs without a word to anyone. He didn't even wait for any of the snitz pies his sister-in-law was serving, but went straight to bed.

Sensing mischief underfoot, John Weaver went out to see who was behind it. His reprimand to the young men lacked conviction, and he came back to the house chuckling. He found Susanna in the kitchen and told her the story in low tones.

"That Johnny just can't keep out of mischief!" she remarked, adding dryly with a smirk, "Well, maybe that'll settle Henry down for a while."

Henry was subdued for the rest of his stay, and the balance of the wedding festivities were carried out with the proper decorum.

On the day of the wedding, benches were set throughout the house in every available spot. The parlor was filled, spilling over into bedrooms and part of the kitchen. Fires had been lit in the summer house where the meals would be served. Young girls with shining eyes and rosy complexions crowded the stairway in colorful dresses like a border of summer flowers. The bride had made herself a dress of royal blue wool; and from now on she would wear the delicately pleated, white organdy cap, and for church gatherings the organdy neckerchief and apron which all married women wore.

Andrew Yoder and his mother had driven over early in the morning. His eyes were on Elizabeth who "sat next" for her sister. Ringlets of gold escaped from under her cap which she had tied loosely under her chin. Her dress was of a slightly lighter shade of blue than Sarah's. Andrew hoped for a chance later to talk to his sweetheart. As the preacher droned on, the young man allowed himself the luxury of thinking about her, contemplating what it would be like to see her eyes light up when he encountered her.

Once during the feast that followed the ceremony, as she sat primly beside Joe who was her escort in the wedding party, Andrew's eyes caught hers for a moment. Her eyes clung to his, caressing him, remembering. A sweet agony of desire swept over him. He determined he would find an opportunity alone with her before the evening was over. Joe gloated jubilantly, but Andrew noted her cheerless face and thought, "He can't make her smile!"

The young waiters came by noisily banging and shaking their tin pans to collect coins for the bride and groom. Andrew dropped in some coins, grabbed his hat and slipped outside. He stood alone on the porch looking up at the soft snow coming down. Darkness had fallen. He and his mother would soon have to start home. Hearing the door open softly behind him, he turned to see Elizabeth coming out, a shawl wrapped about her shoulders. He could picture her coming out this same door last summer, bare feet skipping lightly down the steps. He assumed she was running an errand to the main house, but to his surprise she came and stood before him, looking more lighthearted than he had seen her all day. Their clandestine moment would be short, with people coming and going; and someone was sure to wonder where Elizabeth had gotten to. "Hello, Andy." It was almost a sigh.

Little snowflakes were twinkling and melting on her hair. He saw his own love reflected in her eyes, and seizing the moment, he drew her into the shadows away from the window. His desire made him bold. He held her against his chest, his strong arms encircling her as he bent his head to meet her upturned face. Hungrily his lips pressed hers. He was taken by surprise at his own emotions and amazed at her response. Lost in each other they stood thus oblivious to time and their surroundings. Then he released her, looking hopefully into her eyes.

"Can I come to see you soon?"

"Oh, yes," she answered shyly, quickly.

"I'll be going out west of Millersburg to work at a sawmill, leaving Sunday. I'll stay there most of the winter likely. Saturday evening then?" he smiled.

She nodded, returning his smile. And shaking the snow from her hair, she went inside.

All the way home Andrew and his mother drove quietly through the softly falling snow. She sensed his need for quiet contemplation; he reveled in reliving the exhilarating moment when he held Elizabeth in his arms and in the prospect of seeing her in a few days. Any fears of losing her to another had melted as the flakes of snow that fell on the horse's back. By the time they arrived at home, the snow was several inches deep, and the wheels crunched softly as Andrew drew up at the gate.

CHAPTER VII

Snow kept falling all day Friday. By noon it was up to the horses' knees on the roads. By Saturday morning no one was going anywhere. The roads were clogged with snow so deep that the milk was not hauled to the creamery but was kept in the cool water of the spring house. The newlyweds on their way to visit relatives had gotten as far as Dover where they spent the night with the bridegroom's aunt and uncle. Elizabeth looked pensively out the window at the drifts getting higher and higher. Her hopes of seeing Andrew that night were fading.

By midafternoon the sun came out. Johnny poked his head in at the door. "We've got the sleigh hitched up. Wanna go for a ride?" The snow-covered head disappeared leaving little puddles inside the door.

Elizabeth and Annie didn't need a second invitation and raced out in their mantles and black overcaps to join the other young folks who were collecting from the neighboring farms. Some waded through the snow on foot, and some came in sleighs. One farmer's horsedrawn sled, that was used for hauling logs in the winter, had made a path through the drifts. Shouts and laughter rang through the air as snowballs flew, the girls squealing and ducking playfully.

On a flat part of the meadow the boys tramped a large circle in the snow with a hub and spokes for the game of "fox and geese". The fox chases the geese and when one is tagged, he becomes the fox's helper in running down the other geese. The last goose to be caught is the winner. Joe became the "fox" and stood in the hub with the other players in the outer circle. His determination to catch Elizabeth himself was obvious as he ignored the other players in pursuit of her, but she eluded him for a time.

The others, chagrined at his lack of sportsmanship, turned on him, the geese chasing the fox. Catching him, they pushed him down and washed his face thoroughly in snow. Soon someone suggested they abandon their game and go sleighing.

As the sleigh glided noiselessly over the packed snow, Johnny urged his brother-in-law's team into an exhilarating speed, leaving the girls breathless and laughing. Slowing when the sleigh's runners hit the dry planks of the bridge, he turned the team around, and they sped back, passing other sleighs full of jovial boys and girls. The bridge looked so bright now in the snow, so different from that stormy night last summer when Elizabeth and Andrew had stopped in its shelter. She remembered his protective arm about her waist.

"Penny for your thoughts," Johnny's voice brought her back. "Maybe they're worth more than a penny," he teased.

"I was just thinking," she answered lightly, trying to sound offhanded. "I would like to get off at *Grossmummy's* when you go by, if you can slow down enough," she said in mock annoyance.

"Aren't you having fun?" asked Johnny, disappointed.

"Oh yes," she replied. "I would just like to talk to 'Mummy' and see if she and *Däddy* need anything."

Reluctantly he reined the horses in and stopped at Peter and Veronica's lane. "At your service," he said, bowing with exaggerated gallantry as he helped Elizabeth down.

She walked to her grandparents' home in a flurry of snowflakes. Through the window Veronica had watched her much favored granddaughter wading to the door. She fluttered about her, taking her cap and mantle and hung them by the stove. "Here, sit by the fire and warm your toes."

Peter stirred from his nap and smiled at his granddaughter. "The children are taking a holiday today, eh? Ach well, you're only young once. So why aren't you out there with that young Joe Mast having fun?" he teased; and tapping his pipe on the coal hod, he settled back to refill it for a smoke.

Veronica was small and quick. With decisive steps she bustled about, getting down the flowery, bone china tea set that she saved for special occasions. As she poured steaming cups of tea, the house filled with the aroma of mint she had gathered and dried on sunny summer days. *"Däddy, why don't you go out and have a little fun yourself?"* the old woman suggested. Maybe you can catch a ride down to John's with Johnny." They exchanged glances. "You can bring the milk back, Peter." Her dark eyes twinkled knowingly.

"I believe I will do that, Franey," announced Peter finishing his cup and rising to go. "It will soon be time to feed the horse and, anyways, I'm no good at these fancy tea parties," he said, bending down to pull on his "artics." He stuffed his arms into his coat sleeves, pulled his black felt hat down over his ears and stomped off through the snow, swinging an empty milk bucket from his arm.

Until now Elizabeth had kept her and Andrew's interest in each other a secret except to mention to Susanna that he was coming to see her. Her disappointment grew deeper with each passing hour, as there was less and less hope of seeing him tonight. With her pragmatic approach to life, Susanna would have been satisfied if her daughter had married the neighboring Joe. Veronica was the one to be consulted in matters of the heart.

As soon as they were alone, Veronica, studying Elizabeth's thoughtful face, cut to the heart of the matter. "It isn't Joe you like, is it Honey?"

"No," the girl blurted, "and I thought after tonight he'd quit bothering me!"

"Tonight? Why after tonight?" the grandmother questioned gently.

Elizabeth stared at the roses blooming in her cup. "Andy promised he would come to see me tonight and go to church with us tomorrow. Do you think he can come in all this snow?" she asked, blushing.

The older woman deliberated before answering. "It might not be wise, and Andrew seems like a very sensible young man. If he can't come tonight, there'll be another time."

"But he's starting work next week in a sawmill on the other side of Millersburg, and it will be too far, especially if the roads are bad."

"You don't want to see him just so Joe will let you alone, do you?" Veronica asked simply.

"Oh, no!" came from Elizabeth quickly. Veronica detected the genuine feelings that lay behind the faraway look. She felt the girl's thwarted hopes as if they were her own."If your love is deep enough, it's worth waiting a little," she offered tenderly. "My mother used to say, 'things have a way of working themselves out if you wait a little'. Think how let down Andrew must be feeling if he can't come."

"Oh yes, I hadn't thought of that," answered the girl brightening. "I'd better be going, Mummy, it's time to get supper." She pulled on her outer clothes, peered out the window to make sure no impertinent young man was waiting about on the road, and stepped out into the snow to trudge the half mile home. The shadowy sky brought early darkness, and the young people had scattered to their homes to do their evening tasks.

Andrew sensibly stayed at home and nursed his deep chagrin that his plans had been dashed. On Sunday morning the sun shone from a crystal blue sky. The air was crisp and brutally cold at noon as he saddled his horse. He went to the house to tell his mother good-bye, the snow creaking under his feet. "Well, I'll be going."

Catharina slipped a brown paper package into his coat pocket. "*Mach's gut*," she said, gently pressing his arm. She missed him so when he was gone.

The twenty-some miles to "Spinnly" Joe's place seemed like fifty. The horse at times waded in drifts up to his belly, and sometimes it was difficult to determine where the road lay. On and on he went past empty fields, past woods and scattered farmsteads. The wind died, bringing a stillness as the sun descended with a rosy glow. He whiled away the hours playing an old harmonica he had carried with him since boyhood. A fox stopped in her tracks to stare and to listen, then trotted off into the woods leaving Andrew to his lonely thoughts. He bit into a cold sausage. "Come on, Prince," he urged. "No time for dawdling. There'll soon be shelter for us both." The horse stretched his neck back to nibble the corn bread Andrew handed him.

Coming to the rim of Paint Valley, Andrew stopped to scan the scene. Far beyond a dim light shone from a window, and smoke curled upward from the chimney. Sensing the nearness of his own kind and the shelter they were coming to, Prince whinnied and quickened his steps.

"You're a good-meaning old poke, Prince." Andrew reached up and patted the horse's neck. "But I guess you know if I was pickin' my company for the evening, it wouldn't have been you. No offense. Easy now. You don't want to break your neck when we're so close. Your supper is being made ready at this very moment," he added, seeing a lantern bobbing from house to barn in the darkness below. "Your bed will be ready, and you won't have a worry for many days while I have to work for my living, you sponger," Andrew chided, giving the horse a good-natured slap.

The young man soon felt comfortable in the home of Joe and Mattie Troyer and their six young children. (Though Joe had become a strong and robust man, he had been thin and sickly as a child, and the nickname he had acquired stuck with him.) They both were industrious, she at her housekeeping, and he at his farming in the summer and logging in the winter. Joe expected hard work from his three or four extra men that he hired to work in the sawmill, but he treated and paid them well. Andrew relished the camaraderie of his fellow woodsmen, and the hard labor in the wintry outdoors; felling trees with his ax and bucking them to standard lengths, was to his liking. At night when the men came home, Mattie Troyer and her hired girl had a hearty supper waiting for them. Working in the cold, fresh air gave the men robust appetites for the fried potatoes, ham, sauerkraut and cornmeal mush; and soon after eating, sleep summoned them.

One night that first week, Andrew sat by the lamp after the other men had turned in and penned a letter to Elizabeth. His years away from home had made him skilled at letter writing. Writing to his mother had taught him to fill his letters with the descriptive details of everyday life that women love to hear. His language was simple, not flowery, but he found it hard to express to the girl the things he really wanted to say.

"Dear Elizabeth, I am very sorry that I could not see you on Saturday last. I had really pinned my hopes on it. As you know, the snow was too deep for traveling any distance. I rode Prince out here on Sunday and he waded in snow up to his flanks. It was cold, but I found it enjoyable. It is more wild out this way. I saw minks, muskrats, quails and several red foxes. There was almost no one on the road, only a few sleighs. I wish you could have been with me to see the red sun go down, and how the windows in the houses glowed as if they were on fire. Then as it got darker, the moon shone so brightly you could have almost read a newspaper. It was so still that people's voices and dogs' barking carried for miles. It would have been so much more enjoyable if I could have had you with me. But then we would need a buggy. I would not ask you to ride with me on my horse going that far. The other hands have already gone to bed, and so should I, as there will be hard work tomorrow.

"Thinking of you, Andy"

They were busy at the sawmill. Andrew's thoughts continually went to Elizabeth, but he was not afforded the privilege of a Saturday to go to see her. Doubts began to plague him. Did she think about him? Had their kiss meant as much to her as to him? Would that imbecile Joe beguile her into keeping company with him? No, she wouldn't! But yet the saying was, "out of sight out of mind". His misgivings made him melancholy, until finally a letter arrived from his beloved.

"Dear Andy," she wrote. "I have been staying with Grandmummy since *Däddy* has been feeling poorly and probably will be here for some weeks. Mother had a quilting last Wednesday. There were thirteen women here besides all the children and babies which I didn't count. Mary J. Miller always likes to play tricks on people, but this time the joke was on her. Lydia S. Beiler, who was sitting next to her, sewed her apron fast under the quilt. When Mom called for them to come for dinner, Mary J. got up so fast and pushed her chair back, she almost pulled the quilt down on top of herself on the floor before she realized what had happened.

"Oh yes, the quilt is a beautiful flower garden. Mom says since Sarah already has hers, this one will be mine if I ever get married. It sounds like your work is very hard, and so cold it's been. Take care of yourself.

"Remembering you, Elizabeth J. Weaver"

The letters back and forth were sparse but highly cherished and read and reread until they were dog-eared.

After some weeks of felling and sawing trees, it came time to haul them five miles southeast by horse and sled to the mill at Killbuck Creek.

Here some were made into lumber, and the rest were stacked in huge piles until spring thaw brought the waters up, and they could be floated down to the railyards in Millersburg. The job of taking them to the lumber mill was Andrew's and Mose Kauffman's. Mose, known as "Little Mose" to distinguish him from every other Mose, had a stocky, muscular build and was known for his ability to handle his team of work horses. Andrew was entrusted with Spindly Joe's team of big, brown draft horses.

The temperature was down to twenty degrees when they started out; the sled's runners crunched deep into the snow; and clouds of steam came from the horses' nostrils. The brisk air made them frisky and eager to go. The January sun shone weakly from the wide-open sky, and by noon snow was sliding from the trees. They let the horses rest as they ate their cold beans and thick slabs of cheese and homemade bread with apple butter.

"Joe doesn't trust many to drive his team, but he's glad when he doesn't have to make the trip," stated Mose.

When they got to the sawmill, other hands unloaded the logs, sorting them into piles.

"Here comes that little Irishman they call Snake," Mose pointed to a team and wagon with an indistinguishable, but voluble, blob sitting atop a shabby load of logs. His voice could be heard shouting at his horses before he was close enough to be recognized as a small red-faced human.

"Makes a lot of noise for such a little person," Andrew observed.

"He's been drinking," Mose exclaimed. "He never is entirely sober. Lives a couple miles west of town on a little farm, mostly woods. He makes enough on logging to get him through. I stay away from him. Mean little guy. His wife left him years ago, they say."

"Doesn't look as if he spends much on horse feed," Andrew noted the gaunt animals struggling up the slope toward the mill.

Snake was an undersized figure, grotesque in his large overcoat that he wore like a barrel. In a sudden burst of anger, the veins on his ruddy face bulging, he pulled at the reins and whipped the animals, shouting obscenities to any man or beast within earshot. The confused horses turned and darted downhill toward the stream where they stood trembling, re

fusing to move, unresponsive to their owner's shrieking commands. The sun had thawed the topsoil on the riverbank enough that the heavy load was sinking the iron wheels into the bog so that even had they tried, the brutes could not have budged the weight. Andrew, having drawn closer to see if he might be of help, viewed the development with increasing alarm.

Never known for his good judgment, Snake was at the end of what wit he had and undertook whipping his team across their heads and shouting until sweat stood out on his own forehead. In a flash of disbelief he found himself suddenly lying on the ground, dazed. Andrew stood glaring over him for a moment; then he went to the frightened horses, stroked their noses and calmed them with his voice.

"Whoa now, easy, easy," he gentled them, patting their withers. Unhitching them he led them away leaving the wagon's rear wheels slowly inching down the bank. Snake stood up unsteadily, protesting vehemently and was pulled off backwards by two strong lumberjacks who had been watching the spectacle.

"You haven't heard the last of me!" screamed Snake as he was conveyed to a safe distance.

With deft hands Andrew hitched his employer's draft horses to the wagon. He spoke soothingly, encouragingly to them. Then mounting the unstable pile of logs, he gripped the reins firmly. "Bill, Charley, giddap," he commanded. The horses strained forward, but the wagon did not budge. The young man snapped the reins on the broad backs and sang out, "Come o-on!" Cajoling them, "Yup, yup, yup!" With necks straining and muscles rippling the horses dug their hoofs down and put all their energy into obeying their master's bid. With much creaking and grinding the wagon teetered ominously behind them and finally came to rest on solid ground, but not before the load of logs had shifted and rolled precariously. With an agile leap Andrew had escaped being knocked down and severely hurt. Breathing a sigh of relief, he unhitched the team.

Snake's arrogance had been deeply stung. His insolent tongue had been muffled momentarily, but he did not intend to take such disgrace without retaliation. Grimacing sullenly at his new adversary, he walked hang-dog toward his cowering team without a word of thanks to Andrew, leaving his audience shaking their heads.

Later that afternoon Andrew and Mose drove their teams into town to get some soup and coffee to warm themselves before they started the trek back. There was Snake's team and wagon tied in front of the Travelers' Inn Saloon. Before going in, the two men fed their horses the grain and hay they had brought. Instinctively Andrew offered a handful of oats to each of Snake's two emaciated animals and left a pile of hay for them to feed on.

Inside the steaming dining room the odor of wet clothes and the sweat of working men mingled with the stale smell of fried foods and the smoke from the fires. Around the pot-bellied stove on the dirty wooden floor stood puddles of melted snow. When their eyes were adjusted to the gray indoor light, the two men saw, hunched over his plate of food and fully engrossed in making it disappear, the little man with the big temper.

"Think he's cooled down a little?"

"Looks like the food and coffee might be helping, but let's sit down over on the other side of the stove," said Andrew, pointing to a table where they would be facing Snake's back. "I don't want to tangle with the little varmint again."

"He's no match for you, Andy," Mose chuckled. "I think the lumber hands were a little surprised at you."

"Why for?" Andrew looked puzzled as he sat down.

"Oh, it wasn't that they weren't glad to see him get his due. He's had it coming, and the other fellows put a few finishing touches on your job when they got him up to the mill," Mose chortled. "It's just that, well, us being Amish they kind of expect us to stand back and just let things go."

"You mean because we don't believe in fighting?"

"Yeah, they kinda expect us to be weaklings, let people walk over us," agreed Mose.

"The way I look at it," suggested Andrew, sipping the coffee Nell, the proprietor, had set before them, "it's the weak people who are usually the bullies."

"I think you have it about right," said Mose. "Just like the little.....," he nodded his head in the direction of Snake.

"Yeah, the only way to stop him was to put him out of commission for a little. Didn't do him any real harm," said Andrew resolutely. "Might make him stop and think the next time he feels like mistreating his horses." Mose looked at his friend admiringly.

"The elders say not to fight back, not even to defend yourself," said Andrew, "but I feel that taking abuse yourself is a different thing from rescuing someone else from a tormentor. Even a horse should be defended against such a maniac as he. Sometimes force is the only kind of correction a man like that will recognize."

They bowed their heads in silent thanks over the steaming bowls of vegetable chowder which Nell had brought. The two men ate in silence, and Andrew let his thoughts dwell on more pleasant experiences, happy to put the incident with Snake behind him.

The malevolent little man who had been the subject of their conversation was in a more jocular mood as he downed his last shot of whiskey, pulled his cap down over his dirty, orange hair and stood to leave. He called a cheery good-night to Nell, staggering toward the door in his oversized coat. Before he closed the door, his eyes fell on the Amish man he now considered his enemy, and his mood altered. He moved a step closer, squinting in surprise. "You yellow-bellied bastard, you!" he growled through clenched teeth with a string of oaths, his bloodshot eyes shooting sparks of hatred. "You think you're so good! You might have got the best of me before, but I'm ready for you now," he snarled shaking his fist. His threats would have been laughable if he hadn't looked so pathetic.

Andrew leaned back in his chair, his face passive save for the trace of a smile at the retreating figure of Snake.

CHAPTER VIII

The February nights were still very cold, but the warm sunny days melted the snow on the southern slopes and made the sap run in the trees. Joe Troyer hung his sap buckets on the maple trees, and the logging work slowed down. Mattie spaded a piece of her garden patch so she could plant some early vegetables.

"Ach, it's too soon yet," chided her husband. Nevertheless, she sprinkled the little lettuce and radish seeds and stuck several neat rows of onion sets.

"You can't have too many of them," Mattie contended.

Joe and Mattie's little boys and girls loved to ride along on the big wagon when their father and Andrew went around through the maple bush to gather the sap that had collected in the buckets. They begged to go barefoot, but Mattie insisted that spring wasn't here yet, and the ground was still too cold.

When enough sap was collected, it was cooked in a big vat in the wash house. It had to be stirred and watched carefully for hours, sometimes way into the night, so it would thicken without scorching. Sweet, tantalizing smells drifted on the air. They brought back memories of his boyhood to Andrew, of streams of warm, golden syrup hardened on mounds of clean snow to melt again on your tongue. He was getting restless to see Elizabeth. Sitting in the wash house late one night while Joe kept watch over the steaming vat, and bringing in wood from time to time to keep the fire going, Andrew posed the question of having a few days off to go home. Since the winter work had slowed, Joe was friendly to the idea.

"I should take my horse in to get him shod before I make the trip," Andrew added.

"It's all right. We'll get along here," Joe assured the man he had come to lean on as his most valued hand.

So it was that Andrew found himself back in town on Friday afternoon. Jack Hipp, the blacksmith, had several other horses tied to his hitching post waiting to be shod that day.

"I'll get to it in a couple hours if you wanna leave your horse here. Do you have any other business in town?"

"Yah, a little," answered Andrew, inspired with a sudden thought.

He pulled his collar up against the wind that was turning colder. Strolling down Main Street, he looked in at the shop windows jingling the coins in his pocket. The lamplighter was lighting the lamps a little earlier than usual.

"It gives storm," Andrew noted as he passed him on the street. The prospect of his errand gave him a warm feeling of accord toward everything around him in spite of the chilling wind.

Andrew was drawn toward the small jewelry shop wedged between the larger stores. His people had no need for such useless things as rings and brooches and bracelets, but they did love beautiful things. Scanning the shelves his eyes lit on a row of music boxes. There were fine porcelain ones with dainty ladies dancing on the lids. There were polished wooden ones with exquisite carvings of pheasants, foxes and prancing horses. Indecision held him fast until his eyes lit on a little white porcelain cottage bedecked with roses entwined around the door and doves hovering above. When the tiny door was opened, music floated forth; clear notes in harmony," 'Mid pleasures and palaces though we may roam, be it ever so humble, there's no place like home."

The old shopkeeper raised questioning brows above his spectacles as Andrew set the music box on the counter. It was a frivolous purchase, the amount of three days' wages, but the young man's anticipation of his sweetheart's joy and surprise at such a gift made it well worth every penny.

"Good choice," the old man said, wrapping it carefully in old newspapers and placing it in a box. "Must be for a very special occasion or a very special person," he said with a twinkle in his eyes.

"You could say that," Andrew answered, wishing to keep his secret to himself, and, tucking the package under his arm, he headed for the black-smith shop to retrieve his horse.

Jack Hipp was not an old man; in his late forties he still had the strength of two men. His huge arms swung the hammers easily hour after hour. His green glass eye stared straight ahead, a vestige of the rougher days of his youth. He was a simple, straightforward man who told things as he saw them. The fire was dying down; it was time to close for the night. He gave Andrew a sidelong glance with his good eye as he hung up his apron.

"Be you from these parts?" he asked, turning to scrape ashes over the coals that still glowed red hot to keep them for the morning.

"About twenty, twenty-five miles east," answered Andrew. "Been work-ing in Joe Troyer's sawmill this winter. I'll be headin' home tonight."

"Had the horse long?"

"Four years," Andrew answered patiently.

"Horse was stolen down near Glenmont this week," Jack Hipp said, busying himself at putting away his hammers.

"Yah?" Andrew was beginning to follow his line of questioning.

"Brown riding horse, white star and four white stockings. Just thought you might want to know. They got a posse out lookin' and a pretty good reward."

"Much obliged for the information, although I don't know what I can do about it," Andrew said, handing the man his pay for the shoeing.

The sky had turned black; the storm had arrived. Snow and sleet, driven by a fierce north wind, bit Andrew's cheeks. He hunched his shoulders against the gale and headed for the tavern, giving up the notion of starting home tonight. It would be more prudent to wait for the storm to subside and leave in daylight. In a note earlier he had told Elizabeth he would try to see her Saturday evening. He would have to cut his visit with his mother short.

Out in his small, dilapidated farmhouse Snake O'Toole was just finish-ing his supper of potatoes and cabbage when he heard the clumping of heavy boots on his porch. Holding his lantern high and opening the door a crack, he peered out suspiciously into the swirling snow. The sheriff and his men had been at his house before, checking neighbors' reports of disturbances. Alarmed, he was about to slam the door.

"We need your help, Snake," Tom McQuinn inveigled with his boot in the doorway. Several of the posse were looking through the stables. "You know there's been some horse stealing going on in these parts of late," Tom continued. "Got a thief on the loose. Want everybody to be on the lookout for a brown horse with white legs. Ain't seen any have you?"

"No sir, nobody been around here I know of." Snake opened the door a little wider. "Must be a lot of horses like that!"

"Not so many. There's a twenty-five dollar reward," Ed Fair informed him as they turned to mount their horses.

The last bit of news lit a fire under Snake. Always ready for a little excitement in his drab, lonely life, extra money in that amount set his mean little mind in motion. "I'll pay close heed," he said, closing the door. A simple plan was forming in his brain, and forgetting his supper, he set about immediately to get started.

Andrew took Prince behind the tavern to the livery stables. It meant paying another quarter, but he would not leave his horse tied without shelter on a night like this. He followed the livery boy, Robert, who was bringing in an armload of wood to stoke the fires. Recognizing Andrew, Nell motioned him to a table close to the kitchen door where she kept him supplied with bread, meat and coffee. She gave her guest a meaningful look as the door opened letting in a blast of wind and snow and with them the ill-tempered little man, announcing himself with a hoot and a shaking and stomping of snow flying in every direction.

Nell commandeered Snake to a distant corner of the room, hoping he would not notice his quiet enemy. He was in an exceptionally good mood tonight, she observed. After he had his supper and his quota of drinks, she would persuade him to lie down by the fire and sleep the night away. She didn't waste any sympathy on the man; neither would her compassionate soul allow him to go outside in his stupor and freeze to death. On a summer night she would not have been concerned for him, knowing that even if he fell asleep, his faithful horse would take him home. She had a word with the stable boy who obediently went out to feed and stable Snake's horse.

For Andrew there was a room above the kitchen where the warmth of the stovepipe gave it a cozy atmosphere. As he drifted off to sleep, he dreamed of the music box and the smiling girl who would receive it. Each time he awakened, he invented a new way that the gift would be presented, and each episode ended in a rapturous embrace. When it was yet very early, he awoke to the clatter of pots below and the smells of bacon and coffee drifting up. The bellowing of cattle, impatient to be milked, rang across the fields from a nearby farm. The wind had died, and Andrew was eager to be on his way. But Nell persuaded him to sit down for breakfast first.

Robert shook the grate in the potbellied stove vigorously, and the flames leaped up. From his bed on the floor, Snake sat up with a start at the racket and squinted at the light. He tried to think why he was here. Slowly he remembered. He was on an important quest and eager to continue it. He had a purpose today, a passionate zeal, a foolish notion that he could accomplish anything. He would drive through the countryside, through every street in every town and village until he found that brown horse that was stolen. He rubbed his scruffy whiskers, smiling to himself. In his haste he didn't even notice the quiet young man at the table by the kitchen.

Forgetting breakfast, Snake went out to hitch up his horse. In the dim light that shone through the window, he distinguished immediately that the one other horse in the stable was brown with black mane and tail. He stepped closer and peered at its head. Sure enough, there was a white star right in the middle of his forehead. He bent down and squinted at the slender legs. For a moment he couldn't believe his eyes. Could it be? But of course, where would a thief traveling through end up on a stormy night? He truly was a fortunate man today! "Saints be praised!" he shouted ecstatically, startling the horses who turned their heads from munching hay to stare with solemn eyes at the jubilant little man. He didn't know who the owner, or rather the thief, of the horse was, but he must make haste before he got away.

A short time later the disgruntled sheriff, awakened by a shrill shrieking voice, appeared in his doorway in nightcap and flannels only to confront the familiar figure of Snake.

"Snake, are you drunk again! What are you doing here this time in the morning? You get on home or I'll have you run in," he threatened.

"I ain't drunk, sheriff," Snake objected, blustering and sputtering. "I found the horse, the one that was stolen! You can see it at the tavern. The thief put up there for the night. I'm sure he's still there, but you better scramble before he gets away!" Snake did not want to lose the reward he had coming, having had so much luck up to now.

"What makes you think you have the right horse?" Past experience had taught Sheriff McQuinn to mistrust the man.

"I tell you, it's the one! It's got a star, white legs and all. I ain't been drinking, Sheriff."

Tom McQuinn thought he'd better go have a look. Lights were coming on in the cottages sprinkled along the road as the two carriages rattled their way into town, the sheriff stopping at Bill Byrne's to alert the posse. Other members of the posse on horseback caught up with them as they drove in at Travelers' Inn surrounding the horse in question as he was being saddled by a youth in a black felt hat. The young man stopped whistling, startled by the circle of accusing faces. The sheriff had expected someone very different from what he encountered, a young man from a group of people with whom he had never had any trouble, a people who settled their own differences. Nevertheless he had his duty to perform. The horse did seem to fit the description.

"Hold it right there!" McQuinn ordered as Andrew prepared to mount. "Is this your horse?"

Snake, shocked into temporary silence at finding the thief to be the one man he most wanted to see shamed, and stunned at another piece of good fortune, suddenly found his voice. "Of course it's not his horse! He's the thief!" he yelled, jumping up and down until Bill and Albert restrained him.

"Is this gelding your horse?" Tom repeated.

"Yes, it is," answered Andrew simply.

"How long have you had him?" the sheriff questioned sternly .

"Four years in March," said Andrew, shifting uncomfortably.

"Are you from around here?"

"Salt Creek Township," Andrew answered tersely.

"Is there anyone around here that can vouch for you?"

Andrew shook his head pensively. "Don't really know many here. Joe Troyer out in Paint Valley.... has a saw mill..... and Mose Kauffman."

Snake laughed gleefully. "It's plain to see that that's the horse you're lookin' for, and the thief, too. I've seen him before."

"Do you know this man?" the sheriff asked Andrew, inclining his head toward Snake.

"I saw him on one or two occasions," said Andrew, looking into the mean little eyes.

"He's nothing but a trouble maker," shouted Snake, thinking of his revenge and the cash reward.

"I'm sorry for the inconvenience, but I'll have to hold you on suspicion until we can take you before the magistrate," stated the sheriff apologetically.

Hearing the commotion, Nell thrust her head out the door trying to decipher the proceedings and listened with horror to the accusation. She heard Andrew plead, "You're making a mistake. I'm not the man you're looking for."

"I hope you're right, mister," the sheriff replied, but until you can get some witnesses... we have to hold all suspects. We will take your horse into custody, and I will ask you not to leave town until after you've talked to the magistrate on Monday morning."

"I would like to have my things from the saddlebags," Andrew asked politely but firmly.

The sheriff nodded permission. The deputy pulled out Andrew's clothes and a package from which a few notes tinkled as he handed it to the prisoner. Tom McQuinn had strong misgivings about arresting this man. He had an intuition that this was not the man they were looking for, but horse stealing was a serious offense, and the law must be upheld, so that was settled, done. He ordered his deputy to take care of the horse while he went in for a round of drinks with his group of volunteers.

Nell, regaining her composure, turned to Andrew, "You may stay in the inn until this is over." Her glance fell on Snake prancing gleefully

89

behind the posse. She turned on him indignantly. "You've overstayed your welcome, Snake. It's time you take your hateful little body and crawl on home!" There was such anger in her face and venom in her voice that Snake did not dare set foot inside her door that day or many days after.

Andrew sat in his room overwhelmed with disappointment. How could this have happened? One minute he was happily anticipating seeing Elizabeth again at last, the next he found himself a prisoner, confined to this lonely place not knowing when he could be free to see her. Nell came up and urged him to have some bread and broth at dinner time, but he had no appetite. As dismay turned into anger, he paced back and forth from window to door. Finally he sat down and unwrapped the music box, setting it on the table in front of him and wound the spring. Softly the notes clinked forth, "Home, home, sweet, sweet home."

He longed to see Elizabeth more than he ever thought he could. He had to disappoint her again! Would she ever want to see him again? The chimes seemed to mock him. He opened the window and as he stood looking out, he raised his arm with an impetuous impulse to hurl the music box and send it crashing on the paving stones below. But his saner nature gaining control again, he checked himself. If he could get word to Joe Troyer, maybe he would come down and bear witness that Prince was his horse. But he, himself, could not leave town. Who would go for him? Below him a slight, plodding figure trudged wearily about his chores. Robert! Andrew's face brightened.

If the stable boy was willing to take a message for him, he would do his stable chores and tend the fires. He hastily went to talk to Nell. As was expected, Robert was delighted at the prospect of a change, however mundane. He was quick and dependable, and by mid-afternoon he was back with Joe's reply.

It was a lengthy note. Andrew read eagerly, "As far as I know, that is your horse, but I cannot go to court for you. We are not to resist evil. We are to receive with meekness whatever punishment is measured out to us and rejoice when we are wrongly accused that we are worthy of suffering disgrace for his name. Great is your reward in heaven. As the holy book says, 'Do not resist an evil person. If anyone sues you at the law to take away your coat, let him have your cloak also.' Our people have never gone to law. I'm sure the brothers would agree with me."

Andrew was stunned. He knew that the Amish bishops were strict about not taking anyone to court, but how could they not witness for a brother in such a clear-cut case of right and wrong?

CHAPTER IX

It was Saturday evening, when young men slip out secretly to visit the girls who have caught their fancy. The sun had gone down, but the glow of starlight on the snow lent the fields and buildings an iridescence. Elizabeth now had a room all her own since her sister was married. A girl her age needed a room, Susanna believed, a room where she could have privacy to entertain a suitor without the prying eyes of little brothers and sisters. Susanna had dismissed her daughter to her room where she brooded. Elizabeth heard her mother and Annie in the kitchen below washing up the supper dishes. The special visitor the family had expected had not come. Still the sumptuous meal Susanna had prepared was not squandered. Elizabeth's brothers saw to that.

Why hadn't he come? Was he ill? Had he forgotten? From her dark room the dejected young girl stared out the window where she could view the barns and fields. An owl whirled softly from the trees and settled on the henhouse. Here came Peter and Ben from the barn carrying a can of milk between them to the milkhouse to cool in the trough of spring water. Lamplight from the window below painted the picket gate gold. Surveying the frozen fields and lonely woods surrounding the homestead, she detected a solitary figure moving across the meadow from the west and approaching the gate. For a moment her heart leaped up in joyful surprise.

But no, she knew immediately it was that other one and not the one she so longed to see. Susanna would invite him to stay and send him up to her. Elizabeth turned from the window and fled down the stairs.

"I don't want to see him, Mem." But Susanna was already at the door about to answer the knock.

The girl determined Joe would not have a chance to be alone with her, and pulling the surprised Annie through the door into the sitting room, she engaged her in a game of "fig mill". When Susanna brought the young hopeful in, the girls appeared to be so absorbed in their game that he got only a nod from Elizabeth and a giggle behind Annie's hand. Peter came to the rescue and involved Joe in conversation as he stood warming his hands at the stove.

Soon the family were all gathered, each occupied in some form of pastime. John, in his rocking chair, was absorbed in reading *The Budget*, the newspaper with letters from Amish friends and relatives near and far. The mother knitted stockings, her head nodding betimes. Benjamin and Jacob played at "mumblety-pegs" behind the stove while little Franey looked on.

Joe lost no time in breaking the news he was bursting to deliver. "They say Andy Yoder's in jail down in Millersburg."

Elizabeth almost knocked the corn and beans from the game board, but quickly regained her composure, continuing to move the kernels with an air of nonchalance. Nevertheless her ears were tuned to the conversation.

"What could he have done?" queried Peter in disbelief.

"They say he stole a horse," Joe said, pleased to be the first to divulge such an important item of gossip to them.

John Weaver leaned forward, his paper pushed aside. "Humph! Where did you hear a thing like that?"

"Bubly Sam's Levi. He was down to the courthouse on business and heard it from the sheriff," Joe answered importantly.

"Well, there must be some mistake. You better get the whole story before you spread such a rumor around," John admonished Joe severely, giving him a withering look that dampened any hopes he had of making points with the girl that night. And since she totally ignored him, the boy soon saw fit to take his leave.

The next day at meeting, new information was learned about Andrew's situation. At supper, after the roast beef and potatoes had been passed, John summarized what he had gathered. "Somebody's horse down in Glenmont was stolen. I guess it looked a lot like Andy's Prince. Some body accused him, and the sheriff is holding him until tomorrow. Then he'll have to stand before the magistrate."

"Andy wouldn't steal a horse!" broke in Benjamin.

"It's his word against the other man's," John said resignedly, pain in his eyes. "The truth will come out in the end."

"Can't somebody speak for him?" asked Peter indignantly, his eyes flashing.

John didn't answer, and everyone fell silent, well aware of the teaching of non-defense that their elders held to.

For the first time Elizabeth realized what could happen to Andrew. Even though he was a gentle man, he was not given to letting someone walk over him. She believed he would speak up against a false accusation, whether it was made of him or a brother or a neighbor. Yet as her father had said, "It's his word against the other man's." Anger rose within her at the injustice of it. Surely something could be done! Grandmother always said, "Where there's a will, there's a way."

"I'm going to Grandmummy's now," called Elizabeth to Susanna who was putting away the last of the supper things.

"So soon?" asked Susanna, surprised.

"I want to do the chores for Mummy before dark." Elizabeth pulled on her outdoor apparel, trying not to appear hurried, and started for Peter and Veronica's house, her flour sack of clothes under her arm. The February sun was low in the sky as she bounded through the snow down the lane to the front door of her grandparents.

"Come in once," greeted Veronica cheerfully.

"Give me your egg basket, Mummy, and I'll get the eggs and take care of Molly before I come in," the girl answered.

"Ya, vell," said Veronica and brought the little wicker basket. "You hardly need a basket for all the eggs we are getting, but they're starting to lay again."

Elizabeth pumped water and carried it to the dozen hens and the horse. Grabbing a fork, she cleaned out the stable and put down fresh straw. She poured an extra measure of grain into the manger, and curried the gentle horse meticulously. "Molly, you and I are going on an important errand tomorrow." The horse turned her brown eyes on her and jerked her nose up and down as if in agreement. The girl stroked the velvety nose laughing. Carrying an armload of wood for the fires, Elizabeth went inside where Peter wrapped in a comforter was nodding by the fire. Veronica pulled a chair close to the big, black cook stove in the kitchen for her granddaughter. "Here, you must warm yourself, Lisbet. Now tell me what is on your mind."

"Mummy, you always know when I have something right important to talk to you about." Warming her hands on her teacup, she began telling what they had heard about Andrew; that her father and brothers knew he could not steal another person's horse, and worst of all that no one would come forward as a witness. It was so unjust! "I have a plan, Mummy. Will you help me?"

"What is your plan, little one?" Veronica queried.

"I'm going to the county courthouse tomorrow myself!"

"What can you do? Besides you can't go all that way alone!" the grandmother objected, shocked.

"Mummy, please let me borrow your horse and buggy. I don't want my folks to know. I know a friend who I think will go with me. He will speak a good word for Andy."

"Ya, vell, if you're sure that's what you want to do."

"Thank you, Mummy," said Elizabeth placing a kiss on Veronica's cheek.

Dawn the next morning found Elizabeth stealing down the road in her grandmother's buggy, a quilt tucked around her knees for warmth. Molly's hoofbeats were muffled by the snow that lay packed on the road, and her breath created clouds in the frigid air. The Frenchman was milking his Guernsey and looked up surprised when the girl appeared in the doorway. She did not let shyness stop her but forthrightly gave her report of Andrew's predicament. The account brought Louie to his feet knocking over the three-legged milk stool.

"He needs someone to witness for him that that *is* his horse, and that he is an honest person," Elizabeth finished.

For a moment Louie could not speak, but stared at her, his mouth a circle of astonishment. "We must go and help our friend," he agreed. Let me quickly finish the milking."

"Grandmother sent food along for us. No need to take time for breakfast before we start," Elizabeth pressed.

All the way to the county seat Louie entertained his companion with anecdotes of his youth, of making a living on the farm, and of his beautiful Octavia who had died in the prime of their life. He spoke fondly of Andrew, referring to the time he outwitted the thief. "That young man is a joy to behold," he said slapping his knee gleefully. The exceptional sparkle in her eyes, as he talked of their mutual friend, was not lost on Louie.

Meanwhile, Andrew had been accompanied to the courthouse and sworn in. To be more accurate, he said it was not necessary to swear but would affirm that he would tell the truth since, his people did not believe swearing to be right. If you weren't a truthful man, how would swearing make you any more truthful?

The courtroom with its polished oak benches was filled with spectators, townspeople and others from the outlying area, hungry for a little entertainment on a winter's day. Sheriff McQuinn laid out the events of the past few days.

"It's highly unusual for us to hear a case such as this without the owner of said stolen property present," droned Peter Sullivan, the magistrate who acted as judge. "However, since he has not arrived, we will commence with the preliminaries so that perhaps we can ascertain the guilt or innocence of this young man. It may be that in the meantime said owner will make his appearance. Who brings this charge?" From up behind his waxed desk he peered over his spectacles at the defendant.

"I do, I do," Snake stood up waving his arms and darting to the front. There was a hubbub in the room. "Order in the court," said the magistrate, bringing down his gavel importantly. "How do you know this man?" he asked, not bothering to swear Snake in. The bad-tempered man's reputation was known throughout the locality.

"A few weeks ago at the lumber mill I was mindin' my own business bringin' in a load of logs with my fine team of horses, when this trouble

maker came out of nowhere and beat me up so I was hardly able to walk."
There was a titter throughout the courtroom. "Satiddy mornin' I seen this
horse in the stables down at the saloon. I knew right off it was the one
they were givin' the reward for. Then this thief tries to take off with him.
I mighta' known he was the one." The churlish one paused, scowling.

"All right, Mr. O'Toole sit down," the magistrate interrupted, banging
loudly with his gavel.

"I'm the one who'll be getting the reward, you know," Snake insisted,
his voice a shriek.

"Sit down, I say! We'll have no more outbursts from you!" The judge
was losing his patience.

Arriving at the courthouse, Louie went straight inside while Elizabeth
led the horse to the watering trough for a drink, then tied her to a hitching
post and threw a horse blanket over her back. Entering the back of the
courtroom, she saw Andrew seated calmly before the magistrate with his
back to the audience. His brown hair was slightly disheveled in that carefree way of his. Looking at the strength of his broad shoulders, she was
moved at the incongruity of his woeful vulnerability to such injustice.
She turned her eyes on Louie who was speaking to the bailiff. How she
hoped he could help!

"Since there are no further witnesses, and seeing that the complainant
has not arrived, the court will be adjourned until tomorrow morning at
nine o'clock." Sullivan was about to bring down his gavel when the bailiff stepped up quickly to the bench with a message.

Andrew stared in disbelief when Louie was called on to take the witness stand. How did his friend know about this predicament he was in?
How could he have gotten there?

Louie described in detail the horse he had seen Andrew with last summer. He related how his friend had spent the night with him, and how he
had outwitted the robber who had taken off with his cash. "I think to
myself," he recounted the night, "my friend's taken leave of his senses,
offering the man his horse that way to make off with my money, but very
soon I see the wisdom in it."

The magistrate was caught up in the story and indulged the old man in giving all the rambling details. The audience was leaning forward, straining their necks so as not to miss anything.

Louie continued, chuckling, "Andy advised the robber to kick the horse in his sides to get him to cross the bridge down by the mill. See, he already knew the horse would probably rear, dismounting his rider or would reach back and grab his leg as he had a habit of doing when Andy first got him. And by the looks of things, that's just what happened! The horse left the thief by the side of the road pretty roughed up and came straight back to his owner with the money still in the saddlebags." The old man's eyes twinkled as he looked around at his enrapt listeners. Never having heard the full details of the incident, Elizabeth was filled with pride and amazement at the cleverness of her suitor.

"We will take a ten-minute recess in which Mr. Ravel will come outside and determine if said horse is indeed the one Mr. Yoder had in his possession last summer, "declared the magistrate.

Louie was able to identify the horse without any question, and the court was quickly convened. Snake slouched uneasily in his seat knowing full well his testimony of hearsay rang hollow and unconvincing. The magistrate, who from the start had suspected a motive of vengeance in the surly little man, scolded him soundly for having detained an innocent man and causing an uproar in the village. He admonished him to learn a lesson in character from the one he considered his enemy. Turning to the sheriff he instructed, "Give Mr. Yoder his horse and let him be on his way." He brought down his gavel, and the room became a hubbub.

"Wasn't that something how he fixed that thief?"

"I knew he was someone special all along." This from Nell, who would have been ready to testify on his behalf herself.

Not eager for any publicity, Louie was already out the door followed by Elizabeth. His work done here, he was impatient to get back home to his house and his animals. His cow would need milking again by the time he got his chickens fed and the other chores done he had not had time to do in the morning. The girl, too, felt uneasy about being missed by her family if she got back too late. Until then they would assume she was helping her grandparents.

Andrew, wishing to speak a word of thanks to Louie, pushed toward the door, but was constantly delayed by well-wishers and admirers. He had suddenly become a man of note. He finally made his way outside just in time to see Louie pull out of the courtyard onto the street. He did not recognize the horse, but he noticed the buggy was the Amish type, and he caught a glimpse of a fair young girl inside whose light brown hair was curling around her face under her winter cap. Instantly he knew it was Elizabeth, but it was too late to stop them. He stared after them helplessly, amazed, his heart torn apart with love.

Back at the inn, Andrew could not be persuaded to sit down and eat before leaving, though Nell plied him with delicacies. As he came down the stairs with his things and said good-bye to her, Robert suddenly burst in at the inn door. "They found the horse! The one they thought was stolen. It had wandered off into the swamps down around Wolf Creek. Coupla' fellows were trappin' down there and came across him," Robert said out of breath. "Guess they had a time gettin' him out of there. And actually he had only two white feet," he added.

As Nell whisked into the kitchen to tend to her breadmaking, Andrew heard her mumble something under her breath, "If that troublemaker, Snake, ever shows his face here again...."

Andrew chuckled to himself, but he had no time for gloating. The past was behind him. He was overwhelmed with thankfulness to be out of the dilemma he had found himself in and eager to experience the new path he was starting on, thirsting to drink from the cup that love held out to him. He would not let circumstances get in his way again. Prince sensed his excitement as they started off at a gallop.

CHAPTER X

By late afternoon Andrew arrived at his mother's house. He paused on the porch and looked in at the window. Sitting at the table was his mother, peeling some wrinkly winter apples she had brought up from the cellar. His nieces, Barbara and Katie, and their little brother, Johnny, were clustered around her begging for "snitz" which she handed to them generously. Of course right now she would be telling the story of Paul and Silas, or of the boy who cried "Wolf" or family stories that were told and retold. His mother's face lit up when he stepped inside, and the children clamored for his attention.

"Is that Sam's horse tied in front of John's house?" asked Andrew, kissing his mother's cheek and ignoring for the moment the children tugging at his legs.

"Yes, Sam's Emma is with Mandy," she answered in muted tones. It was not the kind of thing people spoke about without reserve between the sexes or in front of children. "Her time has come, and John went to get the doctor," she whispered.

"Maybe he'll need help with chores and milking," Andrew offered, hoping in his heart he would not be delayed again. He tickled the little girls in their ribs, and they giggled with delight.

"He's only milking three cows right now," she answered. "They've just started coming in fresh. We'll be able to do it. I believe you may have more important business to look after, Andy." They exchanged knowing looks.

"Thank you, Mem, but I don't want to leave the burden on you."

"Ach, don't bother yourself. Sam's Isaac came along with Emma. He helped John before. He probably has the feeding and cleaning all done already. I'll go out and make sure everything's all right." Turning to the children she said, "Put on your coats and boots, girls, and Barbara, you help Johnny." A buggy was heard clattering. "There's John now," she exclaimed, peering out, "and here comes Doctor Morgan right behind him."

"Might I use your buggy tonight, Mem?" Andrew called after her as she went out.

"Sure," she called back. "Take one of those soap stones along to keep your feet warm." He smiled at her concerned regard of him as when he was a little boy.

Pumping water into a basin, then adding hot water from the steaming teakettle that stood ever ready on the kitchen stove, Andrew prepared his bath. He shaved and dressed meticulously, adding a blue silk handkerchief around his neck for the finishing touch.

As he stood outside the barn hitching Prince to his mother's carriage, John stepped out of the house, and Catharina and the children came running to hear the news. "We have a little boy," John announced proudly.

"Can we come in and see it now?" the children begged.

"Yes, but very quietly so your mother can rest." Picking up little Johnny who was whimpering for his mother, John followed Catharina as she herded the children into the house. He turned to wave to his brother. "Good times, Andy, good times," he laughed. Andrew waved back exultantly and slackened the reins, letting the horse take off on a trot.

Yes, he felt, they are good times; births, weddings and courtings, and always plenty to feed their families. The hard work and even the hard times gave meaning to life. There were the fun times, too. It was indeed a good life. He touched the package on the seat beside him, smiling.

The road had gotten soft in the spring thaw. "Come on, Prince. You want to ride while I walk?" Andrew fretted. But seeing how the wheels were sinking a little in places, he decided he'd have to be patient. He still had some daylight time left; he didn't want to get to his destination too early. He would take this time to talk to his friend, Louie, and thank him for testifying in his behalf. He drove past the schoolhouse, then slowly past Weavers' farm hoping for a glimpse of Elizabeth. He passed her grandparents' house and then the mill which was silent, locked up for the night. Turning up the little road that Louie lived on, he crossed over the wooden bridge, grinning as he remembered the robber and his sorry fate. Prince had no misgivings about the bridge tonight. "Sometimes I think you understand more than what you let on, you old fodder machine," Andrew said to the horse affectionately.

As he stepped onto the porch at Louie's, he heard a strange chug-chugging sound that seemed to be coming from the road some distance south of the covered bridge. But he thought no more about it as Louie opened the door, surprised to see him. "Here, have a seat, my friend," said Louie. "It's been a long time since I saw you."

"Has it?" Andrew rejoined. "I sure thought that was you I saw at the trial a few hours ago!"

"Oui," Louie stammered, "I saw you, but there was no chance to talk."

"You hurried out of there so fast I didn't even get to thank you."

"No," Louie objected, "there was no need to thank me. I was glad if I could help out. If it hadn't been for the girl, I wouldn't 'a known about it. She's a plucky one. Has a good head on her shoulders. Pretty, too," he added with a wink, reading the look in the young man's eyes.

"If I can ever do anything for you, just holler," Andrew said as he started to leave. There was that sound again. Louie, hearing it, came outside and they walked to the fence for a better look.

"It's the teacher," said Louie, pointing across the fields to a dark shape on the road in the bottom. "He's driving his father's new Model T Ford. I heard Peter and Dan up at the mill talking about why he brings that automobile around here. He's taken a shine to the girl, you know." Seeing Andrew's face darken, he quickly added, "But she won't ride with him. She has eyes only for one."

"Well, it looks as though he's not going anywhere right now," Andrew said, brightening. "Maybe we'd better go and push him out."

"No," objected Louie, regarding the handsome figure before him, "I'll get my horse, and help him out and send him home. You, young man," he said tapping a finger on Andrew's chest, "have more important things to tend to."

Preferring not to arrive at his sweetheart's covered with mud from head to toe, he took his friend's advice, grateful for his generosity. "Much obliged," he said with a wave from the buggy.

Susanna pulled back the blue curtains discreetly and glanced out as Andrew pulled up and tied his horse at the gate. "She was too tired to go to the husking with Peter and Joe. We'll see if she's too tired for this one," she muttered to her husband.

"Better she makes the choice than us," John answered curtly, going to open the door. He much preferred Andrew to Joe, and was not in as great a hurry to marry off his daughter as was his wife who often remonstrated with Elizabeth that she would be an old maid if she kept on turning away all the suitors who came courting.

"Lizzie, come down here," John called up the stairs, then sat down to chat with their caller.

The two men talked about the weather, the lumber business, the live-stock. Andrew gave Susanna the news of the "little one" at his brother's house. Presently Elizabeth appeared on the stairs. Andrew rose to greet her. The sight of her made him catch his breath.

"Would you come riding with me, Elizabeth?" he asked simply.

"Yes, Andrew," she said, smiling demurely and getting her cloak from a hook on the wall.

At long last they were alone together. He was speechless with grati-tude and wonder. He climbed into the carriage beside her and tucked the robe around their laps. Putting his arm around her, he pulled her close. With his other hand he flipped the reins lightly, and they started off. The horse dutifully stayed straight on the road and kept going until he was ordered to turn or to stop. Thus Andrew gave his full attention to the girl beside him. The moon, in its third quarter, gave light between clouds from time to time.

Andrew's heart was so full. How could he speak the things he had so longed to say to her? He was solicitous. "Are you sure you're warm enough?" "You haven't been working too hard, have you?"

Finally his thoughts found words. Softly he began, "Do you know how wonderfully beautiful you are? I can't believe that in all this world there

106

is one so perfect a creature as you!"

Elizabeth, not used to such elaborate praise, blushed and started to object, but Andrew put a finger to her lips to stop her. "You not only have the kind of beauty that every man dreams of in a woman, yours is much deeper. You are kind and thoughtful and good. Elizabeth, I loved you so much already before you came to the courthouse today."

Her eyes widened slightly in surprise.

"You brought Louie out there to testify for me. Without you he wouldn't have known, and he couldn't have come that far anyway with his old horse." He paused, then continued slowly, "Yes, I saw you leaving with him, and I talked with him tonight. He said it was all your idea. Why did you do it, my sweet Elizabeth?"

She looked intently into his steady eyes. "Because I care for you, Andrew," she answered solemnly. "We all knew you were innocent."

He drew her closer and placed his lips gently on hers for a long sweet kiss. They rode along without speaking, oblivious to where the horse was going, not caring where he took them. They passed the mill, then the road that turned to Louie's and stopped at the covered bridge that spanned Goose Creek.

"I saw something very interesting down here when I was at Louie's," Andrew said finally.

"What was that?" asked Elizabeth, her interest piqued.

"There was a Model T Ford stuck in the road somewhere along here."

"Stuck in the mud?" the girl laughed. "That would be Alfred."

"Oh? How do you know that?"

"Well," she stalled, "He told me he was going to come out and give me a ride one evening. I told him I wouldn't go, but I guess he thought he could talk me into it."

"Yes, there are the tracks," said Andrew. "Poor fellow! He came all that way and then was stuck for a good while, all for nothing. Louie said he would turn him around and send him home," Andrew chortled.

"It'll teach him for putting on airs," Elizabeth thought out loud.

Andrew stopped the horse on the bridge, the hoofs clomping on the mud-caked boards. The spring thaw had sent the water from the hills into the streamlets, swelling the creek so that it tumbled and rushed below them. The memory of that other night flooded their thoughts, the summer evening when they had found shelter there from the storm. They sat in silence for a time, savoring their new found joy. Elizabeth felt as if she were just beginning to live.

Finally Andrew lifted her face and looking into her eyes, whispered, "Will you be my wife, Elizabeth?" His heart beat fiercely as he waited for her answer.

"Yes, oh yes, Andrew," came her reply.

He drew his hand lightly up over her arms, her back, his fingers gently touching her neck, caressing her hair. She melted into his arms. He pressed his lips to hers for a timeless moment. Then he turned the horse and carriage around and took Elizabeth home.

The lamp burned low in the parlor. Her parents had gone to bed in the next room, and the children had gone to bed, except for Peter who was not home yet from the frolic. Shutting the parlor door behind them, she carried the lamp to the kitchen table where they shed their coats and sat with their backs to the glowing stove that had been banked for the night.

Andrew brought out his package and laid it in front of her. She looked at him quizzically. "It's for you, my love. Open it," he urged.

Her hands trembled as she untied the cord and fumbled with the paper. She touched the music box gently, caressing the smooth shape of the roof and windows, the flowers and birds. When she opened the little door, a small housewife stood sweeping the threshold, and the tune chimed forth, "'Mid pleasures and palaces though we may roam; be it ever so humble, there's no place like home."

Elizabeth knew the song well. What's more, she had always felt like that about home. To be where her loved ones were, to work and play together in good times and bad. Now her place would be beside Andrew; they would make a home. Her pulse throbbed with anticipation.

"Oh, Andy, this is the most beautiful thing I have ever owned!" she exclaimed as Andrew smiled down on her.

Their engagement was kept a secret between them throughout the ensuing months. Though many people suspected it; as the custom was, no one aside from their parents, would be told until shortly before the wedding.

CHAPTER XI

In mid-May Andrew helped his brothers prepare their fields for planting the corn and oats. Often on Saturday evenings he hitched his horse to his mother's buggy and drove to the Walnut Creek area to see John Weaver's daughter. They spent their precious hours together, walking and talking, often ending up at the bridge where it was cool and private. Elizabeth amused him by relating anecdotes from the books she had read. He entertained her with music on his harmonica. The cows grazing nearby raised their heads in astonishment when Andrew started to play a fast jig, tapping his toes in rhythm on the wooden boards. Elizabeth clapped her hands and laughed with delight. The tune done, he stopped out of breath and joined her at the opening in the side of the bridge.

"You're the one who wanted to learn to dance!" she teased.

"Oh, it's nothing," he said modestly, resting his arms on the wooden crossbeams. "My cousins and I used to go to the Irish fairs and watch them do their dances. Then we'd go home and practice them. I didn't know if I'd remember them any more."

On "church" Sundays they went to meeting, he in his carriage and she with her family so as not to be unduly obvious about their intentions.

One Friday evening in May, Andrew brought Elizabeth to his mother's house to visit until Sunday afternoon. Catharina was very pleased at the match of her youngest son with the granddaughter of her dearest girlhood friend. "Such an industrious, hardworking girl," she had observed to herself, "und shö' au'. * Funloving just like Franey," she smiled thinking of the pranks they had played as girls. Her son would not be alone after she was gone, and in the meantime would give her more beautiful grandchildren. She had retired early, leaving the young couple on the porch steps

*and pretty, too   111

watching the stars come out. She could hear their murmuring voices late into the night as she finally drifted off to sleep.

Far to the southwest a dark cloud looked threatening, though the rest of the sky was clear. The air having gotten chilly, Andrew wrapped his coat around Elizabeth as she leaned her head on his chest and slept lightly. The delicate scent of apple blossoms was wafted to them on the breeze. Occasional flashes of lightning illuminated the distant clouds with an aerial beauty, lighting her face from time to time. He would have loved to stay thus all night, but he knew they must soon go in.

Suddenly, above the horizon he noticed an unusual glow. As he watched, it grew brighter, appearing as a large, bright star. Soon he could see a long, luminous tail following behind.

Andrew roused Elizabeth with, "Look once, *Liebchen*."

"Wunderbar!" she gasped, rubbing her eyes.

Andrew ran to John and Amanda's house and tapped on their window rousing his brother who came running with his wife behind him.

"Halley's comet," John said briefly, awestruck. "They were talking about it down at the store."

When Amanda saw the wondrous sight, she went back to get the older children. Catharina, too, awakened by the commotion ran outside, wrapping a blanket around her shoulders. "*Ai, es ist!*" she exclaimed letting her sentence dangle in amazement. They all stood for a long time in quiet astonishment as the comet moved slowly across the sky, wondering if it might be a sign of something cataclysmic.

Little Barbara, her eyes large with wonder, expressed their thoughts in childlike simplicity, "Is it the end of the world?"

"No, hush," her mother suppressed her in awed tones. "We must go in now."

Unnoticed, the rain clouds had crept closer. Sudden large drops sent them scurrying for shelter.

"We can use the rain," said John, holding out his hands to let it splash on his palms as he followed his family into the house.

All night long the storms came and went, some only distant thunder bringing gentle rains. Toward morning a more tempestuous storm blew through. The trees bent in the wind and lightning crackled very near with loud booms that rattled the windows. Andrew, who had lain down fully dressed, peered out the kitchen windows trying to assess through the driving rain whether or not any tree or building had been struck. As the first light appeared in the east, the storms moved off leaving the trees dripping, the air fresh.

About to go back and lie down, Andrew caught a glimpse in the semi-darkness of someone coming through the gate in a great hurry. Presently he saw it was John.

"Sam's barn is on fire!" John shouted as Andrew flung the door open. "His Isaac was just here to bring word. Struck by lightning, they think. Are you coming with me? Hurry!"

Andrew grabbed his hat and followed his brother with a hasty wave to his mother, "Don't wake Elizabeth, but tell her when she wakes up." He could see the glow of the fire a half mile away and the smoke rising above the trees.

The men led the livestock out of the barn, putting them into the meadow with young Isaac manning the gate so the animals could not return into the blazing inferno. The fire was gaining ground quickly, flames shooting high into the sky as they caught on the small amount of hay that was still in the mow. Fortunately it was the time of year when most of the grain and hay had been used up, so the loss was not as great as it might have been. There was no use in trying to save the barn. Even now the roof and floors were beginning to collapse. The sight of smoke filling the early morning sky brought people from neighboring farms to help or just out of curiosity. Some were pouring water on the sides and roof of the milkhouse, and a bucket brigade had been formed to save the corncribs. Billows of steam rose into the air from the intense heat.

When the fire had spent its fury, and it settled down like a hungry dog to finish devouring the rafters that had fallen on a fiery heap, Andrew, seeing there was nothing more that could be done, looked around to see who had dared come to help his brother. Besides the family members, there were a few neighbors who were hardly recognizable with soot covering their faces and beards. But no matter that not many had come to help, the fire would have run its course. More people could have made little difference. He was very thankful that his brother's house and other buildings had not been burned. But a new barn would be needed quickly in which to store the new crop of hay.

As Andrew walked home he mused on the barn raisings he had gone to as a boy with his father and brothers. Men and boys would come from neighboring communities far and wide, and, working from dawn until evening, they built a barn from foundation to roof. Often as many as three hundred men came. The women made it an occasion to serve a feast.

But would the Amish do this for Sam who had left the church? Or would they strictly observe the ban of fellowship placed on him in which no one was to have any dealings with him? Andrew's mind was in turmoil. He wanted to help Sam, but he, himself, would be expected to shun his own brother if he wanted to follow the church as he had planned. How could he be a part of a religion that required this? Yet he could not ask Elizabeth to leave her church and be ostracized from her family. It was of course unthinkable for them to belong to different fellowships. He decided not to mention any of his concerns to her, and wait for the time being.

Elizabeth assumed that his quiet, thoughtful mood was because of the shock and fatigue that accompanied the fire. As Andrew drove her slowly back home on Sunday evening, she ventured, "I'm thinking about being baptized this summer."

"That's good," he answered. "I, myself, have spoken to Bishop Kauffman some months ago about joining the church."

Young people routinely asked for baptism if they were contemplating marriage, promising to faithfully keep the ordinances. It meant they were ready to settle down and take on the full responsibilities of family and church life.

"When are we going to be married?" Elizabeth asked shyly.

"When would you like to, Liebchen?"

"Would the end of October be too soon?" she urged. "October is my favorite month, I think."

"Then October it shall be, provided, of course, we have a place to live by then. I'm sure we could stay with my mother for a while, but I want a place all to ourselves," he said drawing her close.

Getting the fields ready for planting the corn kept Andrew busy the last days of May. The warm sun on his back as he walked behind the plow in the cool furrow, the smell of the sweaty horses, the birds singing their nesting songs, the vibrancy of his own body as he steered the plow through the mellow earth, all gave him a feeling of joy in being alive. As he harrowed the fields and then planted the corn, he contemplated his future with Elizabeth, the home they would build together. He rehearsed over and over the plans for their wedding they would plot on one of his next trips over to see her.

In early June the haying began. Andrew raked into rows the swaths that lay drying in the sun. He and John loaded it onto the wagon while Mandy drove the horses and Catharina minded the children. There would be plenty of feed for the livestock when winter came.

One evening after supper, when the first crop of hay was finished, Andrew walked across the fields to his brother, Sam's, to see how he was faring. They stood knee-deep in the overripe clover.

"Well, I don't have a solution for this, brother," Andrew said, biting on a stalk of timothy. "You could still have a pretty good crop if you had a place to put it."

"There's no use cutting it if there's no place to store it," replied Sam, resignedly, stooping to crush a handful of dry blossoms. "I may as well let the cows in here."

"We could cut it and stack it in big piles in the field. It wouldn't be very good hay by the end of winter, but I guess it could get you through," suggested Andrew.

"Yes, I'll have to sell most of my cows, anyhow. I could keep one or two in the buggy shed over winter. I might have enough hay for the rest of the livestock," agreed Sam.

"When do we start? No use in letting this hay go any longer. Send me word when it's ready to rake, and I'll give you a hand."

"Now, Andy, I don't want you to risk your standing in the church for my sake."

"Don't concern yourself about that," Andrew said, dismissing the idea. "We'll need to think about putting up some kind of barn, too."

"Yah, I know. With the money from the cows I could maybe make a start, maybe put up a little shed."

In their hearts they both knew it would be a hard row to hoe. As Andrew walked home in the summer twilight, he wondered how two men could build a barn in time to get the harvest stored. And even if they could, how would Sam get his wheat threshed? It seemed like an impossibility. Without help from his Amish neighbors in harvesting, Sam risked losing everything he owned. And what was he risking everything for? Andrew wasn't sure. For some difference of interpretation that was evidently very important to Sam, or was it a deeper commitment to what he believed? One thing he knew, he had to stick by his brother through thick and thin.

The dilemma of his divided loyalties weighed heavily on his mind. Long after he went to bed Andrew lay awake, staring into the darkness. The bishop had been very firm about his not working or eating with Sam. Perhaps no one would find out about his helping him now and then. Still, as crisis followed crisis, could his help be enough to get his brother through? But how could he not help him? Without a wheat crop there would be no money to pay the taxes and to buy shoes for the children. Yet if he had any dealings with him, even eating at the same table, he would be considered rebellious and would not be allowed to join the church. And marrying Elizabeth meant first joining the church. He couldn't ask her to leave the church with him; her family would have to boycott them then. There seemed to be no answer. Long after midnight he fell into a fitful sleep.

The more perplexed he felt, the more he threw himself into the laborious task of haymaking at his brother, Sam's. With young Isaac driving the team, the two men stacked the dried timothy and clover into haycocks, knowing their work was only a makeshift solution.

High on the wagon's heap, forking the grasses to make an even load, Andrew saw a buggy come around the turn in the road, and as it came closer, he saw it was Bishop David Kauffman. The horse and buggy seemed to him to speed up as it passed the field, but the bishop nodded a greeting in answer to Andrew's friendly wave. "Not particularly neighborly," he thought aloud. "Well, now he knows I'm here helping Sam," he said to himself.

He felt sure that now the bishop would not allow him to be baptized unless he confessed he had been doing wrong and would promise to discontinue associating with his brother, neither of which he could do in good conscience.

The haying was nearly finished when rain came. The remaining rows would have to be turned again to dry in the sun; but that would wait. On Saturday afternoon Andrew hitched up and started for the Weavers' feeling downcast. He would have to postpone marriage plans until the conflict in his mind was resolved. Perhaps they could never be married. There was no solution, only a high wall that he could not surmount.

Sunday afternoon found the young couple walking hand in hand through the country lanes toward the bridge. Elizabeth carried a nosegay of wild phlox and honeysuckle that Andrew had picked along the way. He was quiet, reflective. She sensed he had something on his mind. They entered the cool shade of the bridge, and Andrew lifted her up on the beam that served as a ledge for an opening cut out as a portal. He looked at her tenderly, as she buried her nose in the flowers. How could he tell her what was weighing on his mind? But he knew he must.

"Elizabeth, you know that I love you more than life itself." She smiled, searching his face. "I am not ready to join the church yet," he continued, "which means we cannot be married now."

"But, why...what has happened?" she stammered, alarmed.

Andrew leaned against the king post alongside the opening and stared at the floor. "I need to help my brother. You know the problems he's had with his barn burning. Since he left the fellowship, our people won't help him harvest his wheat and oats, so I helped him last year as much as I could. Dave Kauffman warned me then about associating with Sam, and now this week he saw me over there helping make hay. Don't you understand, dear one, I cannot let my brother down. But I don't think the ministers will baptize me.

Elizabeth looked down pensively at the water below peacefully rippling over the stones. "Why does there have to be all this trouble over people who leave the church? Why do we have to shun these people?"

"I think the bishops are worried because numbers of people have been leaving and joining the house Amish, and so they began to enforce this rule more strictly. But I'm afraid all they are doing is persuading more people to leave," Andrew answered with a tinge of bitterness.

"Are you thinking of leaving our people, Andrew?" she whispered.

"No," he replied quickly, kicking a clod of dirt with his shoe. "I don't want to leave." He paused, his voice breaking. "But my conscience tells me to help my brother!"

Elizabeth picked some petals from her bouquet, dropped them into the current below and watched them float away, swirling among the rocks never to be seen again. "Andy," she began, tears welling up in her eyes, "If you leave, I would go with you, stay with you, no matter what happens!"

As long as they had not made the commitment to the church, they would not have to be shunned by their friends and family, but neither would they any longer be considered a close and intimate part of the group and he perceived how dear their people and their ways were to them, how deep their roots went.

He turned to her, touching her hair, her face. "I cannot let you make that sacrifice. Something will work out for us, Liebchen. But I could not ask you to suffer being shunned by your family for my sake. We must be patient and see what God's will is. I think it best for now." He paused, measuring his words carefully. It pained him so to hurt her. "It would be best if I stopped seeing you for a while. You are free to see others if you wish."

She turned her head away quickly and bit her lip to keep the tears from coming. She knew she could not dissuade him. His mind was made up.

Elizabeth languished through the summer days taking long walks in the cool evenings after the work was done, but finding no joy in the woodland flowers, the birds or the changing sky as she had before. For weeks she hoped for word from Andrew, but none came. Her books, too, held no interest now. She shared her grief only with her grandmother and with her brother, Peter.

She was surprised when Alfred came by one Sunday evening with his father's "horseless carriage". She had walked to the bridge and was on her way back when he overtook her and invited her to ride with him. She was easily persuaded to join him for a ride, not because she was especially interested in the adventure, but because she was glad for a diversion to take her mind off her own anguish. Alfred was extremely pleased, and determined that she have a good time. He pointed out the features of the new machine and even encouraged her to put her hand on the wheel and get the feel of steering it.

"You could learn to drive it!" he urged excitedly. "I could teach you."

Elizabeth laughed at the absurdity of the idea. What need would she have for such a contraption! They chugged merrily along, the wind in their faces. People heard the sound of the engine before the automobile came into sight, and ran outside to stand along the road and stare. Her family, too, were lined up in a row by the gate as the two sped by, her brothers waving their arms wildly, Susanna with her mouth open in consternation. Past the cheese house they rattled, losing speed going up the hill, then turned in at the schoolhouse which was locked up for the summer. Forgetting her troubles, she squealed in delight as they made a rightabout and rumbled down the hill at breakneck speed, clouds of dust behind them. The reckless, funloving side of Alfred, when he was away from his serious duties, intrigued and stimulated her. Elizabeth's laughter made her seem like her old self and was reward enough for Alfred.

Back home they joined Peter and Benjamin in a frolicsome game of croquet until the boys needed to do their evening tasks. Elizabeth went to her room and brought out the last book that Alfred had given her and held it out to him.

"I'm sure you finished it a long time ago," he said, "but I have a couple more for you in my auto. Let me go and get them."

Elizabeth laid her hand on his arm, objecting, "No, Alfred, I can't take any more of your books."

"What, too busy?" he questioned.

"No." She knew she must be honest with him. "You have been such a good friend, and we always have good times, but..."

"Then what is wrong with reading the books I bring you?" he challenged her, studying her face intently.

She paused thoughtfully. "I am spoken for, and it isn't fitting to see you any more," she answered in her direct way.

"It's Andrew, isn't it? Louie told me you and he were keeping company back in early spring. But I was under the notion that you two were no longer seeing each other."

Elizabeth wondered to herself how he had gotten the information. She saw the dejection in his face. She knew she must be firm; it would be unkind to give him hope.

"Whether or not Andrew and I ever see each other again, I have promised myself to him, and I will never love anyone else." She turned and ran into the house, leaving the crestfallen Alfred to gather his books and go home.

Andrew was at home at his mother's. He filled his days with hoeing the young corn and helping care for his brother's livestock. At noon when he came in for dinner, he had no appetite.

"Andy, a hardworking man like you must eat," his mother urged. She sensed that there was some trouble about the girl since he had not gone to see her as he had been in the habit of doing. They had seemed so right for each other.

"I'm not very hungry, Mem," he answered gently.

"Well, I don't know what to make of you, Andy," she said, her voice impatient. "This should be of all times the happiest in your life. Something is wrong!"

"I'm just trying to figure out some things, but don't you worry yourself, Mem."

"What things?" she asked, and he saw she was not going to drop the subject.

"What about Sam and Emma?" he demanded. "Are we to shun them because they have joined a different fellowship?"

"But you can be baptized, marry and go on with your life," she re joined without answering his question.

"If I don't help Sam, how is he going to make it? And if I do, I will have to be shunned, too, if I belong to the church, won't I Mem?" She gave a little gasp, holding the corner of her apron to her mouth. "Oh, Andy, I can't bear to think of it," she said sinking into a chair.

"I could not ask Elizabeth to go through that with her family, too, to not be able to eat at their table or have any business with them."

"If only Sam and Emma would be satisfied with the way things were," his mother moaned. "Everything was so good before."

"Everyone has to follow how they are persuaded in their heart," he answered.

"It's all so 'verhuddled',*" she said in exasperation.

Sorry to have lain his burden on her, Andrew patted his mother's shoulder comfortingly. "Everything will be all right, Mem; don't concern yourself." But he saw tears in her eyes as he went back out to his work.

Andrew sat down on a gnarled root of the old oak tree that had stood in the field when his grandfather was a boy and leaned against its rough trunk. Here he had spent many happy hours of his childhood digging in the earth with an old piece of shard and following barefoot in the cool furrow behind his father. In the stream below he had waded and fished for minnows.

He remembered his mother when he was a little boy, always laughing and ready to do things with him, like go with him looking for tadpoles in the spring. She let him plant his own little garden in a corner of hers, though he seemed to forget it for weeks caught up in all the diversions of a little boy in summer. And miraculously there were always beans and squash to harvest later on. And when she kneaded the bread, her dimpled elbows punching up and down, she let him have a turn at squeezing the soft dough between his fingers to his heart's content. But those carefree days would never come again. After his father died, she had gotten thinner and didn't laugh as much. He knew she looked forward to his marriage to Elizabeth and to the children they would have. Her own mother had died when she was scarcely thirteen years old, and, with eight younger brothers and sisters, her girlhood had not been carefree. She had learned

*mixed up

to accept whatever hardships life brought. Andrew coveted for her a quiet old age enjoying the fulfillment her children and grandchildren brought. Sam's decision to leave the *Gemeinde* had hurt her, and it was plain to see what it would mean to her to have him follow in his brother's steps.

Determined to trust God to work out the problems he could do nothing about, he set about the hoeing with new vigor.

CHAPTER XII

The store in Mt. Hope had had a telephone installed a few years before. All the news that couldn't wait to be sent by letter came and went out of there. Mr. Harold, the owner, usually waited until closing time to relay the messages, but this one seemed urgent enough to warrant shutting up shop to deliver it. Andrew, recognizing the storeman's horse and buggy trotting down the road, ran up to meet him.

"Some of your relatives in Indiana rang up. It's Isaac Yoder. I believe he's your uncle?" Mr. Harold said.

"Yes, yes," answered Andrew impatiently. "What's the trouble? Has something happened to him?"

"Er," Mr. Harold shifted his wad of tobacco. "They said he was in a buggy accident, runaway horse, I think."

"Well, is he...?"

"The funeral will be Saturday. I'm sorry to have to bring you this bad news," said the storekeeper.

The young man's face turned pale. "No. Thank you for your trouble," he said, wondering how he could break the news to his mother.

Catharina was at the door, anxious about what tidings the messenger had brought. She read her son's face before he gave her the full report. She slumped into a chair, covering her face with her apron, and sobbed. After a while she said, "Well, I must go to the funeral. You want to go, too, don't you, Andy? You'll go with me, won't you?"

"Of course, Mem," Andrew said. "If we leave tomorrow morning, we can get there by Friday." He knew there was no question that he should go with her. "How long do you think you'll be staying?"

"When we get there once we'll see."

125

"All right, Mem, I'll ride down to the store and phone to Middlebury. I'll have a look at the schedules and leave a message for them that we'll be at the station at La Grange on Friday.

The mists had not yet lifted when mother and son somberly stepped onto the train, she all in black, and settled themselves for the long trip. Catharina had slept little the night before, and the clackety-clack of the iron wheels soon lulled the distraught woman to sleep. While she dozed, Andrew stood, stretched and wandered down the aisle, steadying himself with his hands as the car rocked back and forth. Train travel was not new to him, and he found the people from different localities fascinating. Here was a man dressed in a bowler and a fine suit reading the morning paper, clearly a businessman from New York or Philadelphia. There sat a woman with a small child sleeping in her lap. Other passengers were having breakfast in the dining car as Andrew passed through.

In the next car a small girl dressed all in black with a large winter bonnet that nearly hid her face caught Andrew's attention. As he drew near he was alarmed to see that her face was swollen and red from crying. He recognized her attire as being that of a very strict group of Amish from their area. Bending down he asked her gently in Deutsch, "What is wrong?" But she turned her head away and continued sobbing.

"Are you alone?" he asked.

Her hands covered her face, but finally her head nodded "yes". He sat down beside her. "Can I help you?" He introduced himself trying to put her at ease. "I am Andrew Yoder and I'm from Holmes County. My mother and I are on our way to Indiana for a funeral. Where are you from and what is your name?" he asked kindly.

Andrew waited. At length, keeping her head bent as she twisted a soggy handkerchief, the girl answered, "We are from Charm. My name is Mandy."

"Who are your parents? It might be that I know them," he questioned.

At this the tears started flowing and she turned away. Andrew could see that she must be in some sort of serious trouble. He sat quietly, and began talking soothingly about himself, his family, his work, trying to distract her. "Did you ever see a dog smile? We had this dog that when

126

we said to him, 'Smile', he would bare his upper teeth just like somebody smiling. His name was Sport." Mandy turned a little toward Andrew, glancing up at him with a glimmer of a smile. Andrew continued, "We could send him after the cows and all we had to do was open the gate. He would round them up and bring them home. He was just a very small terrier, and really no match for those big cows. A kick from one them would have sent him flying. But Sport was brash and bold, and he had those beasts convinced that he was boss and they listened." The slightest giggle from Mandy.

"One winter night the smokehouse caught on fire. We had butchered hogs, and all the hams and sausages hung in there. Dad had fired up a little too much before going to bed, and up at one corner the roof had started burning. Sport barked and barked, and Dad went to see what he was yapping at. He got the fire out before much of the meat was burned. Yeah, Sport was some dog," he ended, pleased with the results his story had had. "Now," he said, leaning toward her, you haven't told me where you are going. Maybe we're going to the same place," he ventured.

"My parents are sending me off to Chicago," she declared without emotion.

"Do you have relatives there, or are you going there to work?"

She was silent for a long while. "No, I don't know anyone there, and they don't want me to come back. They don't care what happens to me! They said I will get killed in the city."

Andrew was dumbfounded. He could not comprehend such a thing, especially not among their people. Was she running away he wondered. "How old are you," he asked.

"Fourteen," she answered.

"I'm trying to think why your parents would send you off to a big city if you don't know anyone."

She stared at her hands, then in a timid voice she said, "They don't want anyone to know about me." Then shyly turning her head in his direction, she said, "I'm going to have a little one."

He sat stunned as the picture unfolded. Occasionally an Amish girl would conceive out of wedlock, but usually with a young man with whom

127

she was keeping company, and so plans were quickly made and they were married. He conjectured that Mandy's parents could not bear the stigma of such a thing, she not being old enough for marriage. Still, how could they disown her so cruelly even if they were very, very strict? Mandy did not appear to him to be wild and unruly. He felt disbelief and anger. How was it possible that Godfearing parents would rate the opinions of others so highly that they would turn in hatred against their own child? He was sure of what he had suspected for a long time, that religion for some people was not geniune but only a cloak that covered an unregenerated heart.

"You must not go to Chicago, you don't have to go!" he said firmly. "Would you like to go with my mother and me to Indiana?"

She nodded her head slightly without looking at him.

"I must go see how my mother is faring. She may wonder where I am. I'll come right back," he said. "Stay right there."

Catharina had not missed her son, but roused momentarily as he came up. "I'm going to stretch my legs a little, Mem," he said as she laid her head back and fell asleep again.

"All right," she murmured.

Andrew was devising a plan, but he could not let his mother in on everything. He must maintain as much secrecy as possible for the girl's sake. He would only tell her that he had met a young Amish girl from their community who was getting off where they were and would need help in finding the friends she was to stay with. He hurried back to talk with Mandy.

"I know some very kind people who live a way south of where we are going. They have always wanted children, and would be so happy to have you for a daughter, I'm sure," Andrew began, sounding very optimistic in spite of the misgivings he had. "You could help Emmy with the house-work and she and Henry would take care of you and your baby's needs. How would you like that?" A hopeful smile crossed her face.

But how would Emmy and Henry feel about having a young pregnant girl dropped on their doorstep? He had not talked to the couple for several years. He knew he was taking a risk, but hoped to God that his plan would work. He could think of no other plan to help the girl. To abandon her was unthinkable. "Now I want you to come, Mandy, and meet my mother, " he said.

She obediently picked up her small bag of belongings. *They probably didn't give her any money, either,* he thought to himself. *Only a one-way ticket to get her out of their lives!* Andrew wondered what they would tell their friends and relatives had happened to Mandy. He was thankful that in God's providence he had met up with her.

Catharina was pleased to have a young girl of their people traveling with them even though it was obvious she was from a stricter group. From her bag of stuff she brought out and unwrapped slices of her home-made bread, cheeses, and baloney sausages which she shared with Andrew and the girl who ate hungrily. The old woman was interested in finding out all about their young friend's people and where she was going, but Andrew ambushed her interrogation, whispering to her that Mandy was shy and very homesick and not up to conversation. At their urging, Mandy lay on the seat and fell asleep, exhausted from days of turmoil, and there she slept until the morning. Andrew, having gotten his mother a berth, lay on the seat opposite Mandy and slept fitfully. He wondered how he would deliver his young charge to the Amish acquaintances who had come to mind when he first thought of a place for her. Should he go to them first and see if they would consider taking responsibility for her, or should he just walk in with her and present her case? Either way he would need to find a ride. He preferred not asking for help where he would have to do a lot of explaining.

When the train stopped in late morning in Lagrange, Indiana, a man of their people was there to take them to the Middlebury community where Isaac's family lived. He remembered him only in a limited way. "What would be the best way for me to get to south of Topeka," Andrew inquired of him.

"Must you go yet today?" the man asked.

"Yes, this young girl that's with us is going to work for some people there, and I want to make sure she gets there all right," Andrew replied.

"Well, there are always people going back and forth. You might be able

130

to catch a ride from somebody."

"In that case, I guess we'll just start walking and see who comes along," said Andrew grateful that the man hadn't asked prying questions. "Thanks for taking my mother to Isaac's place." After explaining to Catharina that he would see her next day, he and Mandy started off on foot.

"The land is flat around here." It was the first thought she had volunteered, and Andrew felt encouraged that her spirits were better.

"Have you ever been out of Holmes County before?" he asked.

"No," she answered.

Not surprised, he wondered if she'd ever been more than twenty miles from home, but he didn't ask her. "It *is* very level here compared to home. It makes for easier farming, though. Look, here comes a wagon. Maybe we can get a ride."

A farm wagon loaded with sacks of grain overtook them and stopped obligingly as Andrew waved to the driver. The driver invited Mandy to sit up on the seat with him, but she preferred to sit in back on the bags with Andrew. So they traveled some miles until they came to a fork in the road where they had to get off. Soon a man in an "English" buggy offered them a ride, and thus, by one form of conveyance or another, they arrived at Henry and Emma Stutzman's farm famished and weary.

Emma, an energetic woman in her early forties, came bustling from the henhouse carrying her collection of eggs in her apron. Flabbergasted at seeing the two, she almost dropped them. "Why, Andy, is that you? What brings you down here? I suppose you came out for the funeral. We just got news of it this morning. Didn't your mother come?"

"Yes, she went on up to Isaac's from Lagrange, and we came straight down here." Andrew knew she must be wondering why he was here instead of with his mother and the other relatives. Aside to her he lowered his voice, "I want to talk to you alone a little."

"Well, come in once," she said affably. You must be tired and hungry. Henry will be coming in from the field before long, and I'll get supper started." Going into the kitchen she brought them each a glass of cool mint tea. She assumed Mandy was Andrew's niece who had come with him and his mother for the funeral. She conducted the girl to a chair by a window where she could observe the outdoors and sip her drink. Emma gave Andrew a look, inclining her head toward the kitchen.

When they were out of earshot, the woman stood waiting, her arms folded across her breasts. He noted her puzzled look. How should he begin? He knew her and her husband only through brief encounters while he lived with his uncle and aunt. They had always appeared to him to be very generous, warmhearted people, thoughtful but not overly strict. As he looked now at the kindly eyes he began to make his request. "This girl, Mandy, is in a predicament," he began in a hushed voice. "She needs a place to stay and I thought maybe you and Henry could give her a home. But I'll wait to tell you the whole story when she's gone to bed tonight."

Completely baffled, Emma lost her voice for a moment. "Sure, y-you go and look after her while I get supper on. I think I hear the horses coming in from the field now."

Later when Andrew told them the girl's story and of how he had found her on the train, the couple were incredulous. "How could any parent do a thing like that? The poor girl! She's just a child herself," said Emma.

"Did she say who the father is?" Henry asked under his breath.

"No, I didn't ask her any questions about it," said Andrew.

Emma bit her lower lip and clicked her tongue. "There'll be enough time for that later," she said.

The two men nodded in agreement. "Right now she just needs someone to care for her," said Henry shaking his head in disbelief. "What do you think, Emmy? Do you want to have a daughter?" he smiled.

"And a granddaughter, Henry, don't forget! Wouldn't that be nice? I'll teach her how to cook and raise chickens and make quilts. You'll be Dad and I'll be Mem." For an instant they forgot that they were not alone. "And soon we'll have a little baby in the house, a baby of our very own!" Emma added, hardly able to contain her excitment.

"But don't forget," cautioned Andrew. "I don't know much about her. Only what she told me. She seems compliant enough, and I hope you won't have any problems."

"Leave it to Emmy," said the husband fondly. "She tames all the wild things around here."

"We'll love and care for her and her little one as we would our own," said Emma. "Oh, the poor thing! She must be terribly frightened and homesick. I think I'll go up and see to her right now."

When Emma had gone upstairs, Andrew said, "It will mean two more mouths to feed, Henry, and more work for Emmy."

"Oh," replied Henry, "my wife thrives on that kind of thing, taking care of little orphaned birds and rabbits. It's the best thing that could have happened to both of us, though a sad thing for the girl.. And no doubt she will be a help to Emmy in time to come."

Emma tiptoed down the stairs smiling, "She's sound asleep, the poor child must be worn out. I'll see to it that she gets her rest from now on, and some proper clothes."

"Now don't you go spoiling her already," her husband teased.

"She can use some spoiling," Emma defended herself. "We'd better all get to bed, too. You two have to start early for the funeral tomorrow. I'll stay home with Mandy."

Mandy was still asleep when Andrew with his host drove out in the top buggy at early dawn on Saturday. He had no opportunity to explain to the young girl that he might not see her again, but felt reassured that Emma's love and solicitude would win her confidence and heal her heartache.

The large barn floor was packed with people from surrounding districts and out of state. On one side on two pairs of chairs rested the home-made coffin. The long service over, the men and boys filed past with somber countenances. Next the women and girls followed in a line, dabbing handkerchiefs at their faces. Last of all the widow and her children stood about it with loud weeping. Then a procession of buggies was formed which solemnly moved forth along a country road. On top of a hill surrounded by farm fields and pasture stood small ancient markers amidst a few trees. Here one generation had buried the one before along with children and youth cut down before their time. Here Isaac Yoder was laid to rest in his prime, just as Andrew's father had been, leaving a grieving family.

As the singers began their somber chants beside the grave, the men and boys removed their hats, and the young gravediggers working in shifts pitched the yellow clods into the cavity, the rhythm of their clinking spades keeping time with the voices.

Winding their way with the other mourners back down the hill, Andrew and his mother walked side by side in silence. They did not need words to feel each other's sorrow. Fresh memories of his father's death came back to them, the loneliness that stabbed like a knife and lay imbedded in the heart, the wound that left a tender scar that never quite healed.

After the simple lunch had been served to the men, and they stood around in groups talking, Andrew ascertained that his uncle's family's farmwork was being taken care of by neighbors. They had brought in his hay, cultivated his corn and relieved the sons of daily chores during this time. Nevertheless, he offered his aunt any help he could give in the weeks ahead. She thanked him saying, "The neighbors have been so good and the boys can handle things pretty well now. I'm just glad you came and brought your mother. She needs you to go back with her."

Andrew found Henry as he was hitching up to go home. "You tell Emma to drop me a line and let me know how it goes with Mandy."

"I'm sure she'll be glad to do that," replied Henry.

"I sure do appreciate you and Emmy taking her," said Andrew. "She would be in a sad plight if you didn't help her."

"We are glad you brought her to us, and you have my word , we will do the best we can and help her, *Gottes Wille,*" promised Henry.

Catharina's mind was full of other things as they traveled home the following week. She asked Andrew if Mandy had found the people she was to stay with. "Yes," he said simply, "she's all set." He felt deeply thankful for good people like the Stutzmans who were willing to help a fellow human in need. What a contrast they were to Mandy's folks. He felt certain Mandy would be all right.

As the train rattled rhythmically along, he mulled over his own problems and the impasse he had come to. If only he could solve them as easily as he had solved Mandy's. There was an ache in his heart for Elizabeth. When would he see her again?

CHAPTER XIII

It was wheat harvest time again, and Andrew had once more hired out as a hand on Simon Coblentz's threshing rig. Most of the time his mind was on Elizabeth. He went about his tasks mechanically, without conviction. He still had found no answer to his dilemma. He felt compelled to help his brother, Sam, some way during wheat harvest. In his heart he was more certain than ever that he and Elizabeth should marry and be together for life. He loved her and ached for her. But he didn't know the answer. One night he took out paper and pen and wrote his sweetheart a note telling her he wanted to stop over to see her when the threshing rig was in her neighborhood. "I have missed so much seeing you these past weeks, I can think of nothing else." He didn't know what he would say to her when he saw her, but he just wanted to be near her after these several weeks that seemed like an eternity. But his words veiled his insecurities. Did she still care for him? Surely she must. Would she settle for....? No, she never liked Joe! Maybe she would be better off with someone else, even Alfred. So doubts and hopes bandied for the young man's heart.

Simon moved the threshing rig to the environs north of Walnut Creek. At Abe Mast's, young Joe watched with anticipation for an opening to have a word with Andrew. His assignment on the stack gave him only a scarce minute or two of respite between loads. When the farmers picked up their pitchforks and staggered to their wagons after the sumptuous noon meal, Joe siezed his opportunity before the machinery was started up. Andrew was busy replacing some small belt or other on the thresher.

"Haven't seen you for a while," Joe began.

Andrew, intent on his work, made no reply.

"You used to hang around this neighborhood a lot," Joe needled. "I guess you don't find it so interesting any more."

Andrew glared at him. "It's obvious you're trying to say something, so why don't you spit it out?"

As small-minded people often do, Joe thought foolishly that by bringing Andrew down he could lift himself up. He pushed on stupidly. "The teacher's been coming around an awful lot with that new car of his. And seems a certain girl really takes a shine to riding with him."

For a moment Andrew felt the sting of the poisonous venom, but quickly recovered. He raised his eyes and looked calmly into his antagonist's. "You are lying, and you know it! It's plain that you don't know what you're talking about."

"But it's true! If you don't believe me, ask Peter," insisted Joe.

"Hold your mouth! And get back to work or I'll lay you flat," Andrew growled as the roar of the machinery began.

With a pompous sneer Joe scuttled off through the straw, gratified in the belief that he had wounded his rival, though he had finally realized that there was no hope for him.

Buoyed by the prospect of seeing Elizabeth, Andrew was more determined than ever to find an answer to his dilemma. They set up the rig at Levi Troyer's to begin threshing the next morning. It was early evening, but Andrew's work was finished for the day. He had for some time been contemplating going to talk to Louie Ravel. Resolving that this was the night, he jumped on his horse and rode over to see his friend. He had not thought of any other man, brother or friend, with whom he could share his misgivings, no one who could give him an unbiased view. In his short friendship with Louie, he had always found him to be straight thinking, a man who had unusual sagacity in ordinary matters. He wondered if now his old friend could give him some wise counsel. Would it be appropriate to go to someone outside his people?

He watched in vain for a glimpse of his sweetheart as he rode by her house. He stopped under the shelter of the bridge, the horse's hooves resounding impatiently on the wooden boards. It was peaceful here. The birds were singing their evening songs in the cattails along the stream. Lilies swayed in the breeze by the road, getting ready to close their petals for the night. Wild roses bloomed in pink and white profusion under the stand of elders and maples nearby. Daniel Weaver's three cows, just let out from milking, wandered to the stream to drink below him. As he watched them, the pungent scent of mint crushed by their feet met his nostrils. How he loved the smells and sights of the country! But his enjoyment was bittersweet now since he had tasted the delight of sharing his pleasures with his dear one. The memories of other times at the bridge flooded back in agonizing torrents. He clicked to his horse and continued on his errand.

The Frenchman rose from his seat on the porch, obviously pleased at sight of Andrew tying his horse at the gate.

"How are you?" asked Andrew shaking his friend's hand.

"Tired," was the succinct reply. "I think I get too old now for such hard work. Pretty soon maybe I have to sell my farm," he added.

Having weightier matters on his mind, Andrew did not take note of the old man's words. As they sat and talked, Andrew came quickly to the point, sharing his thoughts and feelings of the past weeks. He hoped for some affirmation of the path he felt he must take.

"How can I disown my own brother when he has done me no wrong? How could I persecute him in the same way some of our Fathers years ago were persecuted by other religious people?" He stopped, afraid his impetuousness might have offended his friend, but Louie's understanding look encouraged him to continue. "How can I in good conscience become a part of such a thing? Yet I can not ask Elizabeth to leave her church and family. Must I break her heart and tell her we won't be married after all?" His thoughts tumbled forth as a deluge after a summer storm ending in a stifled sob.

Louie shook his head with empathy. Having lived with Andrew's people most of his life, he knew their flaws as well as their merits. With quiet deliberation he gazed out at the horizon for some moments. Finally he answered, "Your church and my church are people. Not perfect, but many good people. Good people," he mused. He continued reflectively, "You must follow your heart, my friend. Marry your beautiful girl. Time will take care of the other things, and you will have no regret. You must first be true to yourself."

The old man had articulated precisely what Andrew's native reason was trying to tell him. He suddenly knew without a doubt what was the right thing to do. Louie had said the other matters have a way of working out in time. He would do what his heart told him to do. He would join the church, marry the girl he loved, and if his brother needed help, he would give it. The rest was in God's hands. If he was shunned for doing what he felt was right, so be it!

"Thank you, my friend. You have helped me see things more clearly." His heart felt lighter now, but it was still to be seen if Bishop Kauffman would baptize him. He determined not to let doubts fill his mind again.

Then suddenly he remembered. "Did you say something about selling your farm, Louie?"

"Could it be you are looking for one?" asked the old man, a smile playing around his mouth. "I would be very content to see you have it, to raise your family here where my Octavia and I lived so many happy years."

"I have saved a little money over the years, but I'm afraid not enough to buy your farm," replied Andrew, stretching out his hand from right to left to indicate the land in question.

"Do you have enough to build yourself a house for you and your new wife? I will live in this old house; you farm my land and give me enough to live on, and when I die, it will all be yours."

"Oh no, we couldn't, you are too generous," objected Andrew.

"But it would make me very happy," insisted Louie. "To have my land producing crops and to have you and your family close by would bring me joy to the end of my days. I have no one to leave my things to, and you are like a son to me. Your bride, I would be proud to have her for my daughter."

Andrew was filled with excitement at the idea his friend had proposed. He pictured himself planting the fields and looking after the animals, while Elizabeth tended her garden and a little flock of chickens. He was bursting to share the idea with her.

"Well, Louie, I'm going to talk to Elizabeth about this very soon," said Andrew. "I'm sure she would be thrilled if we could find a way to do it, and we are very much indebted to your kindness." He shook the old man's hand and stood to leave. "I'll be back to talk with you again soon."

CHAPTER XIV

Elizabeth was spending most of her summer at home helping her mother with the gardening and housework. Though she was never one to shirk her duty, her mother noticed that she was often quiet and lost in her own thoughts, forgetting her tasks. The fact that Andrew Yoder hadn't come to see her daughter for some time was inconsequential to Susanna. There were plenty of other young men. She certainly hoped, however, that the teacher would not be back with his noisy, stinking machine! Besides, he was not one of their people. At any rate, the threshers would be coming to their place in a few days, and there was too much to do to fret about such things.

Getting letters in the mail was still a novelty, and when John Weaver came into the house after the noon meal one day waving a letter in his hand, the whole family gathered around. He slit the envelope with his jackknife and handed it to Susanna.

"It's from Aunt Lizzie. She is going to Somerset, Pennsylvania, and wants me to go with her," Susanna read, "I am to take the train tomorrow and she will get on at the Canton station. She doesn't want to travel alone. Just because she has nothing to do, she thinks no one else does!" Susanna sniffed.

"It would be nice for you to go and visit some of our relatives once, Suzie. You've been working hard. It would give you a little rest," said John.

"Hah, a little rest, waiting on Lizzie hand and foot! Besides, we've got the threshers coming in a few days. She sure gives a person a lot of notice." Susanna bleated.

"Maybe Elizabeth could go," John suggested, half in question. "But

143

you need her here to help with cooking for the threshers."

Susanna contemplated his idea for only a moment. "Maybe she *could* go. I can get along somehow here. I suppose I could get Eli Mattie to help. What do you think, Lizbet?" Susanna asked, and without waiting for an answer, it was decided then and there that Elizabeth would go.

"Aunt Lizzie wants to stay for a month. I suppose Elizabeth could get work out there as a hired girl," Susanna said to John.

"But Mem, I don't think I ..." Elizabeth tried to give her opinion.

"It would do you good," Susanna interrupted. "You've been moping around here for weeks. You'd get to see new people."

"What's wrong with Henry? Why doesn't he go?" demanded John.

Susanna read, "She only says, Henry isn't good enough to travel.' You know she never could read or write very well. She is going to stay with Noah and Malindy Eash. Malindy was Hafer Mose's daughter. She is my second cousin, you know. And they have a son, Jeremiah, who would be about twenty-one and a daughter, Barbara, that's your age, Lizbet. I haven't seen them since they were babies. Go and ask Mummy for her suitcase and get your clothes together. Right after noon tomorrow, Dad or I will take you to Beach City. There you'll get on the trolley and go to the station."

Elizabeth obediently left for her grandmother's. Maybe it *would* do her good to go away a while. At least she could talk to Mummy about it.

"I know what Mem thinks. She thinks I'll find someone else that I will like and forget Andrew. But that will never happen," she said to Veronica.

"Come, dearling," the grandmother soothed the girl patting her cheeks. "Just be patient. I'm sure things will work out for you, sooner than you think. Aunt Lizzie likes pampering, but there'll be other people to help with that," she added encouragingly. "And before you know it, you'll be back home again."

"It'll be the longest month of my life," Elizabeth fretted.

As long as she was at home, at least Andrew knew where to find her if he came to a resolution. She suddenly wished for a few of Alfred's books to take along to while away the hours, but put that thought aside.

The next day just as Elizabeth was saying good-bye to her father and getting on the trolley to meet her Aunt Lizzie, her brother, Peter, was at the mailbox picking up a note addressed to Miss Elizabeth Weaver in a masculine scrawl. He was sure it was from Andrew and sure that his sister would have died to get the note. What could be done now? She would be on the train by now. He ran after the mailman's buggy and begged him to wait while he ran in and got the address changed on the envelope. The mail carrier, suspecting it to be a very important letter, pulled his horse up short to wait obligingly, and the note was sent on its way.

That evening Peter hustled through his chores and hurried off to Hershberger's. He knew Andrew and Simon would be setting up to thresh next day.

"Howdy," Andrew looked pleased to see him.

"We got your note today, that is, I think it was from you, for Elizabeth, but she's not home," Peter stammered trying to get everything out at once.

Andrew's face went a shade paler. Surely they hadn't opened her mail, he thought. "Well, where is she?" he asked impatiently.

"I sent the note on to her right away. She only just left today, for Pennsylvania by train. She's going to be there maybe a month with some relatives, Noah Eash, near Somerset," Peter's words tumbled over each other.

"A month?" Andrew was crestfallen. "How is she, Peter?" he asked simply.

Peter shrugged his shoulders. "She's... quiet, not laughing as much as she used to. I wish your letter would have come sooner."

Andrew shook his head and looked down at the gears he was oiling. "Thanks for coming over and letting me know, Peter," said Andrew, feeling a bit shaken, but not wanting to show it.

"Elizabeth confided in me about what has been going on with you," said Peter. "It spites me that things keep going wrong for you two. She really cares about you, Andy."

Andrew looked up from his tinkering with the belts. "Things are going to start going right from now on," he said fervently. "Peter, do you think you could help Simon run the machinery for a couple of days?"

"Sure," said Peter, eager to be of help.

"Here, you probably know most of this, but let me show you what you need to do each day." And Andrew gave Peter a thorough lesson on how to keep the equipment running smoothly. "Suppose your dad could spare you to work with me tomorrow on top of the machine? By the end of the day you will know everything."

"I think so," answered Peter. My job is usually to help load the wagons in the field, and there are plenty of others to do it."

"If you can take over, I'll go home and get my things tomorrow evening," said Andrew.

"Are you going to see her?" asked Peter, incredulous. Pennsylvania seemed like such a long way off.

"That's what I told her in my letter, so that's what I'm going to do," replied Andrew.

Elizabeth watched, fascinated with the farms and little towns that sped by, while Aunt Lizzie sucked on horehounds and mints and dozed betimes. At the train station in Somerset, the two women saw a row of carriages waiting for people, but one was an Amish surrey, and Aunt Lizzie said that would be Noah Eash whose mother-in-law, Fannie, was Lizzie and Veronica's cousin. She lived with her daughter, Malinda, and her husband and two children that were still at home.

The buggy step was high and Noah agreeably pulled up to a platform made for the convenience of people getting into their carriages. Even so he had to push Lizzie from behind, and Elizabeth pulled from inside to squeeze the rotund woman into the seat, where she sat panting. Then off to his home where they went through the process again, only in reverse. Poor Noah, being a rather small man, fell down and Lizzie on top, but he freed himself and was soon on his feet, and with Elizabeth's help, they got the woman up.

The Eash family was congenial and hospitable. Malinda had prepared a big "company" dinner of fried young chickens, mashed potatoes and all the fresh trimmings from the garden. Barbara and Jeremiah came home from their work and joined the others around the table and were duly introduced.

"Your mother and I are second cousins," Malinda said, addressing Elizabeth. "We knew each other as girls. We lived in Ohio then. We were back to visit my relatives once years ago. I think it was in ninety-one, wasn't it Noah? You children don't remember that, I'm sure."

"Mem said she hadn't seen your younger ones since they were babies," said Elizabeth.

Fannie and Aunt Lizzie were having their own conversation about their acquaintances of years gone by, whoever came to mind. "Amos died, you know, and Mattie stayed on in the *däddy* house, but now she's married to Pitt Sam's Joe."

"Some of his children moved to Oklahoma, didn't they?"

"His one son did. They lived in a sod shanty for a while, maybe still do."

Malinda brought her visitors current about their family and had to know all that was going on in the Weaver household.

"Our oldest daughter is married to Atlee Stutzman, that's Atlee E. They live on the next farm over, have five girls and a boy three weeks old. The older girls are a lot of help already; the oldest is nine. She had a hired girl for two weeks and still needs help. I thought maybe you would like to help out while you're here, Elizabeth. Barbara is promised to our other daughter after next week."

"Yes, I guess I can if I'm not needed here with the extra work for Aunt Lizzie," Elizabeth answered absentmindedly.

"No, there won't be that much extra. But we'll wait until next week, anyhow. Now, who's ready for some raisin pie?"

"Oh, I'm too full. Well, maybe just a little slice."

"Maybe another piece of that chicken first."

The atmosphere was so much like home, the conviviality, the feasting and the plans made around family and church. Jeremiah lost no time in inviting Elizabeth to their singing Sunday night. Of course his sister would be going, too.

"Do you have square dancing after yours?" Elizabeth asked.

"We have playing, but nobody knows the dance arrangements. Do you?"

"Yes, a few."

"Good! Then you can teach our young people."

147

"Oh, no! I couldn't. I'll teach them to you here, then you can be the caller and teach the rest," said Elizabeth. "You have to have a fiddler, too."

"We can never learn it by this Sunday, Jerry," said Barbara, "but maybe in a couple weeks at the next singing."

"Yah, you're right. We three will do a lot of practicing between now and then," agreed Jeremiah smiling at Elizabeth.

Elizabeth was thinking of someone else who wanted her to teach him the dances. She wondered where he was. What was he doing and thinking? She felt so far apart from him. "I think I will go to bed now," she said.

"So soon. It's still early."

"The train journey really wore me out, you know," she answered.

She stretched out on the bed and savored the quiet away from the chatter, luxuriating in hopeful fantasies of being with Andrew. Not in the mood for talking, Elizabeth lay very still and pretended to be asleep when Barbara came up later.

Soon she began to feel very much at home with this pleasant family. Malinda said to her husband one day, "That girl really takes a hold of work. She sees what needs to be done and gets busy before you tell her what to do. She'll make somebody a good wife."

"Not like her great-aunt that she's named after," Noah laughed. "She's a real nice girl."

"I think Jerry's taken a liking to her," said Malinda.

"I'm sure that suits you just fine," teased Noah. "You'd have them married off in no time. But there'll be a lot of other boys taking notice of her, too."

On Saturday evening Andrew was at home again. "I came to pick up some fresh clothes, Mem," he announced to his mother.

"Well, is it a special occasion?" she asked hopefully.

"I'm taking a little trip on the train. I'll only be away a few days," he answered.

"Oh," she exclaimed, bursting to know the details, but not wanting to pry. "You surely won't be traveling on the Sabbath, will you?"

"Well, I'm sure you wouldn't want me to. I was told there's a train going east early Monday morning."

"You're not going to Indiana then?"

"No, there's someone I need to see in Somerset County," answered Andrew.

"What about the threshing?" she asked, wondering if he might be looking for work out there. "Doesn't Simon need you?"

"It's probably going to rain anyhow, Mem. Don't you think it looks like a rainy spell coming?" Andrew remarked facetiously.

Catharina peered out at the sky. There were a few white clouds, but no sign of rain. She let the matter rest.

On Monday afternoon Elizabeth was helping clear away the dishes in the summer kitchen. "Here, let me take those peelings out to the pigs," she offered.

"Yes, Jerry can show you where the pen is. Otherwise, you could just follow your nose," Malinda laughed. "Here comes Jerry now with the paper, and he has a letter. I wonder who that could be from," she said wiping her hands on her apron.

The young man examined the masculine handwriting, then handing it to Elizabeth announced, "For Miss Elizabeth Weaver."

Elizabeth almost dropped her pan of scraps when she saw the familiar scrawl. This was so unexpected, yet so wonderful. She wanted to be all alone to read it in private.

"Jerry, you run that slop down to the pigs," commanded his mother, and Elizabeth followed her inside.

Slipping away upstairs, her heart pounding in her throat, she tore open the envelope and read the short message. "He's stopping over to see me at home, but I won't be there if he comes!" she thought. "He's missed me," she said to herself, tears dropping on the page in her lap. She stood and looked out the window wringing her hands.

"I know what I must do," she declared resolutely. "I'll take the train and go back! Mem said Aunt Lizzie could find someone else to travel back with her. I'll see if she will lend me some money. Andrew will be threshing in our neighborhood this week and will probably come over to our house one evening, and I want to be there when he does. Oh, I've wanted to see him so much! They'll be threshing our wheat on Tuesday or Wednesday, and he's sure to be there then. I will go. Tomorrow morning. I can get Jerry to take me to the station before the work begins. I wonder what Malinda will say. She wants me to stay pretty badly. And what will Mem say when I get home?" she mused. "I don't care. I will go!"

The rest of the afternoon she was in a fog of disbelief and excitement. She would wait until evening to ask Aunt Lizzie for the money. Maybe she would understand and not make a fuss. "After all, she is Grandmummy's sister," Elizabeth thought. She helped get the supper on the table, but Malinda noticed she was very quiet and self-absorbed. The girl hadn't given any clue as to who her letter was from.

Near the end of the meal, there came a light tap on the door. Heads went up questioningly. "Wonder who that could be." Noah went into the sitting room to answer it. He didn't recognize the young man who stood there hat in hand, but knew immediately he was one of their people by his clothes and his speech.

Elizabeth heard the man introduce himself, "I'm Andrew Yoder. I'm looking for Elizabeth Weaver. Am I at the right place?"

"Yah, vell, I suppose it's the same one," Noah stammered.

But Andrew had walked across the room to the kitchen doorway where Elizabeth had run to at the first sound of his voice.

"Elizabeth!" He wanted to clasp her in his arms. "I'm so glad to see you," he said trying not to lose his decorum.

"Andy, what a surprise! I-I wasn't expecting you," she answered with equal propriety, though her eyes betrayed her heart's elation.

"Make yourself at home," said Noah to Andrew, and motioning to the others, "I think these two might like to be alone," he shuffled them into the kitchen.

"Let's go out walking a little," Andrew said, taking Elizabeth's hand and moving toward the entrance.

"That would be lovely," she said shyly, still stunned by the turn of events.

They walked for some minutes before either one could speak. Looking up at the mountains that surrounded the green valley, Andrew began, "This is beautiful country here, and it looks like they'll have a bountiful corn crop."

"I got your note today. Why did you come, Andrew? And how did you find me?"

"Peter sent my letter on. He told me where you had gone. I got him to take my place if they do any threshing. I came because I said I would come, and I couldn't wait any longer to see you."

They had stopped under a grove of beeches. "How has it been for you, Beth?" He had only to look into her eyes to see the answer. "Oh, my darling, I'm so sorry I put you through this. Can you forgive me? Do you still love me?"

"I'll never love anyone but you, Andy," she said, her face upturned toward his. "I've missed you so, and I'm so very glad you're here."

He grabbed her waist and drew her fiercely to himself. "Nothing is ever going to separate us again as long as we live, my dear one." He pressed his lips to hers and held her for a long moment.

"I'm so happy, Andy," she whispered at last.

"You get your clothes packed tonight. We have to meet the train at six o'clock tomorrow morning."

"Tomorrow morning?" she questioned laughing.

"You and I, we have a wedding to get ready for," he smiled as they started back.

She would tell him later about the plans she had made before he arrived.

On the way home, as the train rocked back and forth in a gentle rhythm, Andrew told Elizabeth about the proposal Louie had made to build themselves a house, and farm his land on shares until he died when it would become theirs.

"I want to build us a house, but maybe that won't be right away."

"Where will we live, Andrew?"

"We'll work something out. I'm sure we could live with my mother, but I'll need to be on our farm to take care of things and to get the wheat planted. I do hope we can have a place all to ourselves. We'll see. The end of October, isn't it?" He gave her a wink. "That gives us three months to get ready."

"Three long months," she responded.

"But I'll come and see you often," he promised.

Then reaching up suddenly and touching his face, she remarked smiling, "You didn't shave, Andrew."

That's part of getting ready, too," he grinned knowingly. "It takes time for that, too," he said, referring to the custom that required young men to let their beards grow at the time of their marriage.

It was pleasant to watch the scenery from the windows together. They observed the hills getting smaller as they neared home. Andrew had borrowed his mother's horse and buggy and left them at the livery. Elizabeth was anxious that her mother might be angry that she came home and left Aunt Lizzie.

"You leave that to me," Andrew assured her.

Peter ran up to them as they drove in. "How did the threshing go?" Andrew asked.

"All right," answered Peter. "Tomorrow we're to thresh at Hochstetlers'. Then we'll pull the rig over here. I'm really glad you're back! I have a lot of things to learn yet."

"Work with me a few more days, and you'll be ready to take over next year if you want to work for Simon," said Andrew.

"Aren't you going to go with the rig next year?" asked Peter.

"No, I'll be workin' for myself," said Andrew with a grin, lifting Elizabeth down. Annie, Joseph and Benjamin ran to her, excited to see their sister, and led her into the house, full of questions about the train trip.

John Weaver sauntered over, and the two men shook hands. "I'd like to have a word with you and Susanna for a minute if I could," said Andrew.

"Yah, vell," said John. Then, "Mem, come out here once," he called loudly, and Susanna popped out the door eager for an accounting of what was going on.

"I'm sure you both would like an explanation," began Andrew.

"Huh, to say the least!" Susanna replied.

"Now, give the young man a chance." John nudged his wife.

"I had planned to come and see Elizabeth this week, but she left before she got my note, and Peter sent it on. I told her I was coming to see her, and I'm a man of my word. So, well, I brought her back with me, and I, want to marry Elizabeth," Andrew said, his voice firm and controlled. "I have asked her and she has consented. We are not staying apart any longer."

"We wish the best for you both," John answered. "I have seen how you work, and am sure you'll be a good provider. Our family regards you very highly and welcomes you."

Andrew had a sudden uneasy feeling about things as yet unsettled, but pushed the doubtful thoughts away. "Well, I'll be going. I have to be back at Hochstetler's bright and early in the morning," he said, giving the reins a flick. "And I'm looking forward to having some of your good cooking the day after," he remarked to Susanna.

"Oh," she faltered, but recovering quickly, called after him, "Stay over with us Saturday after the threshing and have Sunday dinner."

The next days were sweltering. Wheat harvesting was coming to an end for another year. After the threshing at Weavers', Elizabeth ran out to catch a moment with Andrew as he and Simon got the machinery ready to chug to the next farm. Standing a little way off so as not to seem too obvious, she laughed with delight at his dusty arms and the greasy smudge on his handsome face which was beginning to sport a very appealing fringe along the jawline. He smiled back at her hair going every which way in the wind and the way her skirts clung to her legs. Joe, leaving, took a farther way around, pretending not to see them. Though Andrew went on with his tinkering, Elizabeth felt his total awareness of her. "I'll come around Saturday evening, early," he said.

She answered with a little nod, then tripped lightly toward the house as he stood to watch her go. Feeling his eyes following her, she turned at the door and gave him one quick, flirtatious glance.

Sunday was the alternate day when church was not held in the Troyer district. Only the necessary work of caring for the animals and cooking for the family was carried out. It was a time of gathering together, visiting, resting and quiet recreation. Peter and Veronica Miller's clan of children and grandchildren met at John and Susanna's for a feast, notwithstanding the bounties they had been indulging in during threshing the past week. Susanna was in a more festive mood than usual. "We must use up the leftovers from threshing," she rationalized. In the afternoon the young children amused themselves with dolls and sticks and balls. The boys went swimming in the mill pond, their shouts mingling with the clink of horseshoes as the men tried their skills on the lawn. Later in the day, before the chores had to be done, Daniel and his wife, Katie, brought a tub of ice from the ice house for Susanna to make her delectable frozen cream dessert, and everyone seemed to appear from nowhere to get their share of the delicacy.

Andrew watched for a chance to talk to John Weaver. When the two men were alone, he took the opportunity to speak to him. "Louie Ravel has offered us his farm for a small share of the proceeds from the crops, enough for him to live on, provided he can live there the rest of his life."

"Yah? You mean he'll give it to you!" John was duly surprised, and pleased. "Well, Louie is a good man and easy to get along with."

"I've found him that way. I just wanted to get your idea before we go ahead."

"I'd say that was a very good proposition! The only thing is, get it in writing so there won't be any problems later, you know, with his church or with his relatives. Though I don't know of any family."

"Another thing," Andrew continued, "he suggested we build a house for ourselves. The old house would be too small for all of us."

"Yes it would," John laughed, gratified with the turn of events. "I think it has just one bedroom. But even a big house is sometimes too small for two families. The Frencher has lived alone a long time, too, and this way his life won't be disrupted." John Weaver stroked his beard. "Yah vell, as soon as we get the wheat and oats in, we'll get started." He paused, seeing Andrew's quizzical look. "Oh yes, we help our children get set up. We've got plenty of logs already dried out and stacked in our woods, and we'll have a house up and ready to move into in time for the wedding, providing it isn't for a couple months," John finished with a teasing look in his eyes.

Families often gave their children livestock, a new carriage, furniture or even a farm if land was plentiful. Andrew had not anticipated such generous help as Elizabeth's father was offering. He went to find his betrothed to tell her the exciting news. They would not do business on the Sabbath, but one evening they would talk to Louie and get everything in order.

CHAPTER XV

The few weeks of oats harvesting over, Andrew went home. Catharina met him at the door with news. "Word is going around they are going to have a barn raising for our Sam," she said excitedly.

"What do you mean, 'word is going around'?" Andrew queried

"Well, it wasn't announced in church, but John heard it from Pitt Joe's Eli."

"When is it supposed to be?"

"Tuesday in a week John said, *Gottes Wille*," answered Catharina.

Someone, only God knew who, was spreading the invitation around to all the outlying districts. Andrew stroked his chin thoughtfully. "That is real good news, Mem, but I'm not getting my hopes up. I'll wait and see how many show up for it. Has Sam got his wheat cut?"

"He cut it and has it in shocks still out in the field," she answered, looking anxious. "He's talking of having sale and selling his livestock, his wheat, and maybe even the farm."

"But people know he's up against it, and he won't get much for any of it," replied Andrew. "Who's going to buy it? The same people that are the cause of him having to do it in the first place!" he scoffed bitterly. "Well, I have work to do," and he walked out the door, not mentioning where he was going.

He went directly to his brother Sam's to assess the state of affairs. Indeed with the help of Emma and young Isaac, the wheat had all been shocked and stood in neat rows waiting for threshing.

"What's this I hear about our people building a barn for you?" asked Andrew.

"Yes," replied Sam. "Joe Hochstetler was here to look things over and

157

asked me how I wanted it built, so I guess it's really true."

"Jake Isaac's Joe?" asked Andrew.

Sam nodded. "He's the overseer at most of the barn raisings."

"Mem said you were thinking of selling everything."

"If I get a barn soon, I can get my wheat and my second crop hay in, and I think maybe I won't need to sell."

That's good, if it happens." Andrew was skeptical. "In any case, your wheat isn't threshed yet."

"We'll see what happens," answered Sam confidently.

When the morning of the barn raising arrived, Andrew was on the scene early to see the master builder and his crew already at work since daybreak. By the time the foundation was finished, men and boys were arriving from all directions in buggies, wagons, carts and on foot bearing their tools. Women came bringing boiled eggs, cheeses, hams, mountains of loaves of bread and snitz pies, pickles of all kinds, apple butter and cream for the coffee. Andrew watched, stunned, as the framing went up; and men, their sleeves rolled up, swarmed all over it, lifting and hammering the skeleton into place.

"Did you come to stand and watch, Andy, or are you going to help get this frame up?" said a voice.

Could it be? Andrew turned his head. Yes, it was Bishop David Kauffman motioning him to a place beside him to help the row of about two dozen brawny Amish men lift a piece of framing to its place on the side of the building. Andrew jumped to attention, putting his muscles to work with a light heart. There was little time for conversation, and no need for it, as everyone did his job with speed and skill following the direction of the overseers. The spectacle resembled a hive of bees, each doing his assigned work in cooperation. All day Andrew worked alongside his fellows, and as he observed the bishop doing his share and directing others, he had a strong suspicion about whose scheme had gotten this whole affair going.

When the last shingle was on the roof, and the last man had left, Andrew approached Sam. The brothers stood gazing at the magnificent new structure and grinned at one another.

"Shall we put in hay tomorrow or thresh wheat?" Andrew offered.

Sam shook his head, speechless, tears welling up in his eyes, overwhelmed with gratitude. Andrew wondered if his brother wouldn't change his mind now about leaving the church. He knew where *he* stood. Surely there were no better people on earth than their people.

Louie had been right. He had said,"Follow your heart. Time will take care of the other things." Andrew felt a deep serenity and was ready to give all his attention and time to creating a place for himself and his bride. John Weaver brought a sawmill in to his woods to saw the logs into beams and studs. The already dried lumber was hauled to Louie's farm, and soon on a knoll overlooking the valley, a sturdy house began to take shape. Stones from the area formed the foundation. Andrew attached a spring house to the kitchen and piped in fresh spring water which flowed from farther up the hill, so that Elizabeth would never need to pump water or carry it far. The overflow from the trough would be piped to the barn and the chicken house.

Andrew was now spending all his time there and had put a cot in the new house. With the team of Belgian horses he bought at an auction, Andrew plowed fifteen acres and put in a crop of winter wheat for the next year. Saturday when he went home, his brothers presented him with a young draft mare and harnesses and a handsome new buggy.

The young couple would receive a handmade china cupboard from the Weavers. The grandparents were giving them a kitchen stove from Sears and Roebuck. A new four-poster bed from Andrew's mother would be delivered by a local craftsman in time for the wedding.

Elizabeth busied herself with sewing plain, blue curtains for the windows and getting the hen house ready with new straw spread on the floor and in the nests. Susanna would give them a few hens that along with Louie's few scraggly ones would provide them with eggs for the winter. Then there were new clothes to be sewn for the women and girls including a wedding dress and a new white cap, starched and delicately pleated for Elizabeth.

Andrew along with a few other youths from his respective district were baptized. The Sunday after he received the rites, he went to the Troyer

district meeting to see Elizabeth receive baptism. The wedding date was set for the last Thursday in October. A few weeks before, the "Stecklyman" came to see Elizabeth's parents to make a formal proposal of marriage. Peter and Benjamin again drove through the countryside inviting their friends and neighbors to the festivities.

Johnny Miller surprised everyone by showing up a few days before the wedding with a new bride of his own, a young girl he had met somewhere in the West; and who, judging from her lack of cape and apron, had not joined any church yet. The women's tongues wagged. "Wonder where he got *her!*" "Well, maybe he'll settle down now." But Elizabeth saw that Johnny was very happy. Uncle Henry and Aunt Lizzie, of course, appeared early not to miss any of the festivities. He eyed Johnny suspiciously and kept his distance, but Johnny had a new reason to be on his best behavior. Andrew's brothers and sisters with his adoring nieces and nephews joined in the celebrating. Sam and Emma were there with their children. Andrew pondered his brother's relationship with the other people and how he should conduct himself in his presence. He was incredulous when he saw David Kauffman and Sam conversing like old friends. Before the noon meal Catharina found a moment with the bridegroom.

"Sam and Emma have made things right and are back in the church," she said.

"Is that right?" he answered, reflecting her relief. He sincerely hoped they had not compromised their true convictions just for peace.

When the second day of feasting was almost over, but the merriment was still going strong among the young, Andrew drew Elizabeth out a back door unnoticed; and they slipped out to their horse and buggy that Johnny had hitched up and held waiting for them. They sped from there in the cool autumn night. Peter was waiting at their new house with the fires lit. He took the horse and carriage to unhitch, leaving Andrew free to lead his bride across the threshold. Peter kept a watch on the road so that no shivaree serenaders came by with their noisy tin pans and kettles to disturb the young couple.

At last they were alone. He led her through the house surveying each corner of every room, feeling the warmth of the oak furniture, reveling in the comforts they would enjoy. The house smelled of new wood and varnish. He showed her where just a few days before he had finished piping in the spring water and held a cup under the cold, splashing spate for her to taste.

The lovers chose to spend their first three days and nights alone before they would dutifully begin their jaunt to visit relatives in the outlying areas. He chided her playfully betimes that she had not taught him the dances. When the first blissful days had passed, he said with a sigh that perhaps they'd best get started on their trip.

"Must we ?" she asked.

"It's kind of expected, you know. Peter and Johnny are doing my chores so that we can go," he answered.

"But couldn't they do your chores just as well if you were here? Couldn't we go next spring after the roads are better?"

Her reasoning flooded him with delight. "Then you'd rather stay home?"

"Please, Andy."

"I'd rather, too, *Liebchen,*" he said, drawing her to himself and kissing her.

Smooth on their bed lay the cheerful, flower garden quilt. Elizabeth set the music box to chiming on the shelf and came to Andrew hiding her face for a moment on his chest. They felt each other tremble as he held her close. "How beautiful it is," she whispered.

"It's better than I even dreamed," he answered.

They lay in each other's arms until the fire died down, thankful to be in their own house among their own people. This was home, sweet home.